A CARAVAN FROM HINDUSTAN

A Caravan from Hindustan

The Complete Birbal Tales from the

Oral Traditions of India

JAMES MOSELEY

Produced by Summerwind Marketing, Inc.
Telephone/FAX: (888) 820-8140
moseley@wwdb.org

To order additional copies of this book, contact:
Xlibris Corporation
1-888-795-4274
www.Xlibris.com
Orders@Xlibris.com
30643

CONTENTS

VOLUME 1:
THE NINTH JEWEL OF THE MUGHAL CROWN:
THE BIRBAL TALES FROM THE ORAL TRADITIONS OF INDIA

Preface: How I Wrote the Birbal Tales 17
Introduction: The Real Akbar and Birbal 19
The Ninth Jewel 23
How Akbar Met Birbal 24
Mahesh Das Seeks His Fortune 26
The Justice Bell 30
Birbal the Judge 32
The First Case: The Mango Tree 34
The Second Case: The False Mother 37
The Third Case: The Shape of a Diamond 39
The Fourth Case: The King's Mustache 42
The Queen's Plot 44
Birbal and the Pampered Queen 47
Gallows of Gold 50
The Soup of the Duck 52
The First Prize 55
The Patron of the Arts 57
Fate 60
The Donkey's Haircut 62
Birbal and the Persian Shah 66
Cats 68
Birbal and the Seller of Oil 71
Currying Favor 74
Greater Than God? 76
The Swindling Sadhu 78
Birbal and the Crows 81
The Thief's Stick 83
Neither Here nor There 85

Heaven's Gifts 87
The Egg Hunt 88
Birbal and the King of Afghanistan 90
Birbal's Journey to Paradise 92

VOLUME 2:
A CARAVAN FROM HINDUSTAN:
MORE BIRBAL TALES FROM THE ORAL TRADITIONS OF INDIA

The Search for Birbal 97
A Sound Investment 102
Birbal the Historian 104
The Imperial Mangoes 106
Feast for the Lazy 108
The Emperor's Dream 109
The King's Seal 110
The Wicked Judge 115
The Milk Pond 118
The Queen Is Punished 121
Eggplants 124
The Rug Merchant 125
Birbal's House 128
Good News and Bad News 129
Life 131
The Suit of Armor 134
A Child's Whim 136
Horse Sense 138
An Endless Tale 140
The Sword of Adversity 143
The Donkey 146
The Prince of Kashmir 147
The Emperor's Parrot 149
The Caged Lion 151
The Fools' Tax 153
The Miser and the Poet 155
The Obedient Husband 158
The Hunt 160

VOLUME 3:
A COMPANION TO THE KING:
STILL MORE BIRBAL TALES FROM THE ORAL TRADITION OF INDIA

The Caravan of Fools 165

Who's Luck? 170

The Witness of a Mango Tree 172

The Test 175

Checkmate 177

The Courageous Cheat.. 180

Akbar Decides To Become a Hindu 183

The Loan 185

The Heart's Desire 188

Birbal's Khichdi 190

The Mind Reader 194

Caravanserai 196

Slave and Master 198

Sleight Of Hand 200

Banishment 201

The Blind and Those Who Cannot See 203

Ending Evil.. 205

The Mother Tongue 206

The Philosophical Servant... 208

A Fair-Weather Friend 210

The Tibetan Monks 212

Loyalty 215

The Practical Beggar 217

The Golden Touch 219

The Pilfering Tailor 222

Akbar Proves a Point 225

The Loveliest Child 227

Why the River Jumna Weeps 229

The Legend of Birbal Endures.. 230

The End of Birbal 231

Endnotes 233

DEDICATION

To Madlene, my bride, altogether lovely.

To our crown jewels, Natalie, Christopher, Jamie, and Sasha.

To my Mother and Father, givers of dreams and encouragement.

TESTIMONIALS

"Absolutely beautiful. I can see why you have a devoted following."
Duval Y. Hecht, President, BOOKS ON TAPE, INC.

"I have read Moseley's *Birbal Tales* and must say I was utterly enchanted. The stories are beautifully retold in a style that is not only charming in English but could have come straight from a collection of Persian tales at the Mughal court. Moseley has certainly captured the fantasy court world in which stories of this type are usually cast. He continues in the finest tradition of the Mughal *qissagu* (storyteller). I trust he will offer more volumes in this collection to the undoubted delight of his readers."
Wheeler M. Thackston, Professor of the Practice in Persian and Other Near Eastern Languages, HARVARD UNIVERSITY

"At a time when thousands of intellectuals and professionals are migrating from India to the USA in search of wealth, Moseley has traveled to India to collect priceless gems from her immortal tradition and folk wisdom. Devoid of any high-sounding Brahmanic dogma, these tales have entertained and taught people of all levels for hundreds of years. Rendered again in the most lucid style, reading these tales is like reliving one's childhood. The book will fill the void for Indians now living in Diaspora and will give a new dimension of India to its Western readers."
Ved Prakash Vatuk, D. Litt, Director FOLKLORE INSTITUTE, Berkeley & Former Professor of Folklore, UC Berkeley

"Delightful!"

Swapna Vora, Editor, INDIAN EXPRESS,
North American Edition

"It is so rare to have a book that will charm children, please adult readers, satisfy curiosity about foreign folk tales, and inform any reader regarding a different culture. But here is a book that does it all."

Ted Maas, ALLIANCE HOUSE, INC.

"James Moseley's collection of Birbal tales capture the wit and wisdom of the famous Indian courtier while maintaining the simple poetry of those told orally for generations across India."

Maryann Mahajan, INDIA POST.COM

"Moseley's . . . prose evokes the magical world of Akbar's court . . . in witty, charming stories, which are still popular with children in India. Historical notes are appended."

From BOOKLIST

"There are so many wonderful books for very young children, but there is too little good literature for "middlings" from age seven to eleven. This book, which adults can enjoy as well as children, brings praises from a Harvard Professor to a Hollywood Producer. Interestingly, although the tales are indeed charming and amusing, they are not fictional, but true stories of a wise man who really lived in long ago India in the palace of the Emperor Akbar. Birbal served his Emperor with wit and wisdom, and he became so renowned that even today parents and grandparents use these clever adventures as morality tales."

IndoLink.com

"These delightful fables sparkle like Kipling's Just So Stories and The Arabian Nights. They're full of humor and surprise endings. I loved them! The Birbal Tales are perfect bedtime stories—for the whole family!"

NORTH CAROLINA PILOT

"Traveling throughout India for many years, the author collected many tales from the oral tradition surrounding the 14th-century Great Mughal Emperor, Akbar, and his wise advisor, the commoner Birbal. These short stories include clever judgments and sortings out of injustices that Birbal makes, from the familiar Solomonlike offering to cut a precious but disputed tree in half so neighbors can "share" to his tricking of greedy or grasping relatives, jealous wives, or dishonest merchants . . . readers may often guess the solution to a knotty problem before Birbal reveals what happened next. Unfamiliar titles are italicized and footnoted, and historical notes tell about the real Akbar and Birbal. These stories read well as single tales but taken as a whole, they introduce to Western culture one of the best-loved figures in the folklore of India."

From SCHOOL LIBRARY JOURNAL

"Jim Moseley's adaptations of the Birbal classics of India are some of the most delightfully entertaining and inspiring stories I have ever read. Each one is surprising, spun with brilliant wit and ironic twists. They contain important, timeless morals that are refreshing in our contemporary culture of relativistic values. Jim has done us a valuable service, and I look forward to watching their huge success."

Phil Snyder, Actor, Writer, Producer

"I wish you the very best for your new book. Birbal stories are a personal favorite of mine and have been listening to them since I was a child. I am sure you will find a big demand among the million-strong Indian Diaspora in the USA."

**Achal Madhavan,
VEDAMS BOOKS INTERNATIONAL, New Delhi, India**

"I have been waiting for a book like this for a long time."

Mahi Khan

"All the stories are superb."

Viswanath Sanghamithra

VOLUME 1

The Ninth Jewel of the Mughal Crown:
the Birbal Tales from the Oral Traditions of India

PREFACE

HOW I WROTE THE BIRBAL TALES

I was twenty years old when I first went to India. On my first night in Bombay, my good friend Krishna Kotak told me the first Birbal Tale I ever heard. Ten seconds after he finished, its subtle wit burned like a slow fuse and then went off, and I laughed aloud.

I asked for another.

He told me another.

I asked if he could recommend a book of Birbal Tales. He told me there were some comic books and small collections, but said they weren't terribly well written and didn't convey the living humor that came with hearing them over dinner or at Grandma's knee.

So that night at the Taj Mahal Hotel, I wrote down every word I had heard. And thus began a quest of many years and literally from one end of the Subcontinent to the other. Whoever I met, old or young, low or high, Member of Parliament or *chowkidar* (night watchman), I asked all if they had a favorite Birbal tale—and every time I wrote it down.

When I had gathered eighty stories (and could find no more), I began a study of the historical context in which they took place—the fantasy world of the magnificent Mughal Empire. I wove the fables into a sequence that harmonized with the true events of the lives of the Emperor Akbar and his witty advisor, Birbal, for both were real people.

I sent the results for review by experts in the fields of Indian folklore and Mughal history to make sure that the details were accurate. For example, you don't want Indian characters in the sixteenth century sipping tea, when the British imported tea from China to India only in the nineteenth century!

I am especially indebted to Wheeler M. Thackston, Professor of the Practice of Persian and Other Near Eastern Languages at Harvard University and to Ved Prakash Vatuk, D. Litt., Director of the Folklore Institute and former Professor of Folklore at UC Berkeley.

I wrote this book first of all for myself, because I could not find any book that captured the wry characters of Akbar and Birbal as you hear them in conversations with the good people of India.

Then I wrote them for my children, who have grown up on them.

Now my heartfelt wish is that Akbar and Birbal may give to others the enchantment they gave me in bringing them to life.

INTRODUCTION

THE REAL AKBAR AND BIRBAL

B irbal is surely one of the best-loved figures in the folklore of India. For generations the Birbal stories have delighted children and grown-ups alike, from one end of India to the other.

Jalaludin Mohammed Akbar Padshah Ghazi, Emperor of India, ruled from 1560 to 1605. Akbar was great in an age of great rulers: Elizabeth I of England, Henry IV of France, Philip II of Spain, Suleiman the Magnificent of Turkey, and Shah Abbas the Great of Persia.

Akbar was chivalrous and just to all, but he could be violent and overmastering, if needed. His magnetic personality won the love and affection of his people and the respect and admiration of his enemies.

Akbar was superb at riding, polo and swordsmanship, and he was a crack shot with a musket. He was courageous, often fighting personally in the heat of battle. He was a brilliant general, a master of speed, surprise, and minute details. His lightening conquests of India, from the Hindu Kush to Bengal, were feats of military genius.

Akbar worked hard at the trade of king, sleeping only three hours a night. Although he could neither read nor write (he was probably dyslexic), he had legions of scholars who read to him aloud. His son, Prince Sultan Salim, later the Emperor Jahangir, wrote that no one could have guessed that Akbar was illiterate. He loved religion, philosophy, music, architecture, poetry, history and painting. He forged an Empire that enjoyed long-lasting peace and high cultural refinement.

The Empire of the Mughals was vast and fabulously rich. Akbar's lower taxes and rising conquests created prosperity for the people and floods of treasure for the Crown. European visitors estimated that just one province of Akbar's Empire, Bengal, was wealthier than France and England combined.

Birbal was born to a poor Brahmin family of Tikawanpur on the banks of the River Jumna. He rose to the exalted level of minister (or "Wazir") at Akbar's court by virtue of his razor-like wit. He was a good poet, writing under the pen-name of "Brahma," and a collection of his verse is preserved today in the Bharatpur Museum.

Birbal's duties at court were administrative and military, but his close friendship with the Emperor was sealed by Akbar's love of wisdom and subtle humor. In Birbal the young King found a true sympathizer and companion. When, in an attempt to unify his Hindu and Muslim subjects, Akbar founded a new religion of universal tolerance, the *Din-I-Ilahi*, or "Divine Faith," there was only one Hindu among the handful of his followers, and that was Birbal.

Many courtiers were jealous of Birbal's star-like rise to fortune and power, and, according to popular accounts, they were endlessly plotting his downfall.

The character of Akbar in these stories is rather fanciful, and, historically, Birbal is scarcely heard of. Village storytellers probably invented many of these tales over the ages, simply attributing them to Birbal and Akbar because their characters seemed to fit.

Akbar's court was mobile, a tradition handed down from his nomadic ancestors, the Mongols of Central Asia. (Mughal is Urdu for Mongol.) The Emperor ruled sometimes from the fortress of Agra, sometimes from the noble city of Lahore. In the period of these tales, 1571 to 1585, Akbar held court in the shimmering pleasure city which he had built for himself—Fatehpur Sikri.

THE NINTH JEWEL

Very long ago and far away, the Great Mughal Emperor of India died, leaving Throne and Crown to a thirteen-year-old Prince named Akbar.

Bold and intelligent, the boy had to battle fierce enemies to defend the vast kingdom that his father had left him.

But when peace at last shone across his beautiful dominions, Akbar brought to India a Golden Age.

The young King allowed all people to worship in their own ways. Subjects of every color and tongue stood equal before his Throne. Akbar loved poetry, painting, and architecture, and he brought the wisest and most talented men he could find to the Imperial Court.

Nine of these exceptional men were so gifted, so rare, people called them *"Nava Ratna*—The Nine Jewels of the Mughal Crown"—for their value was above rubies.

One of them, Tansen, was a singer so skilled that candles burst into flame at the mystical power of his song. Another, Daswant, was a painter who became First Master of the Age. Todar Mal was a financial wizard. Abul Fazl was a great historian, whose brother, Faizi, was a famed poet. Abud us-Samad was a brilliant calligrapher and designer of Imperial coins. Man Singh was a mighty general. Mir Fathullah Shirazi was a financier, philosopher, physician and astronomer.

But of all Akbar's Nine Jewels, the people's favorite was his Minister— or Wazir—Birbal: the clever, the generous, and the just.

How Akbar Met Birbal

Birbal, whose name means "strong, brave warrior," was actually born with the name of Mahesh Das. He was still a young boy living in the country when the tinkling of horse bells, the thunder of hooves, and the flash of magnificent turbans signaled the approach of a Royal hunting party.

Akbar, who was still a very young King and loved sport, had ridden long and hard with his companions without finding any game. Seeing the skinny lad by the wayside, the Emperor called out:

"Is there a village nearby, little man, where we can water our horses?"

Mahesh looked at the elegant cavalcade fearlessly and said:

"At our house we have a tank full of fresh, cool water . . ."

Akbar swept the boy up behind his saddle, and all galloped away in the direction Mahesh indicated.

The little boy drew water for the horsemen with great courtesy and speed. The King was impressed. When his turn came to drink, Akbar took the bowl from Mahesh's little brown hands and, looking straight into his eyes, asked:

"What is your name?"

"What is your name?" smiled Mahesh. "If you can tell me that, you deserve to learn my name."

Akbar dropped the bowl, and the fresh water vanished into the thirsty dust. Nobody dared to speak to the Emperor that way.

"Do you know who I am?" spluttered Akbar.

"Yes," said Mahesh mildly. "But I'll wager you do not know the name of the Brahmin in our village. So where then is the greatness of kings?"

The noblemen sucked in their breath with horror. They looked expectantly at Akbar, and he scowled back at them. Then the Emperor's gaze met the shining black eyes and quizzical half-smile of the tiny country lad . . . and all he could do was laugh.

"Little man, you are right to remind a king that he should not be proud. I see you have a bold heart and a wise mind. Here."

He took a costly ring from his hand and gave it to the boy.

"When you are grown, present yourself, with this ring, at my Court. I will remember you, little brother."

And, leaving the boy to ponder the wonderful ring, the Imperial hunting party cantered off.

Mahesh Das Seeks His Fortune

W hen Mahesh Das became a young man, he took the few coins which were all his savings, along with the royal ring, kissed his mother farewell, and set out upon the long road to the great new capital of the Empire, Fatehpur Sikri.

Never in his country childhood had he imagined so many people as he found in this splendid city. Mountains of sweets, colored golden, green, and red, were sold in the bazaar, along with precious silks, elegant lambs' wool hats, and gold jewelry hammered as thin and fine as a feather. Mahesh was amazed. He felt as though he could wind through the covered alleys and wide streets for months and never see the same thing twice.

Huge camels glided past, water-sellers gave their nasal cries, acrobats and magicians attracted small crowds, incense spiraled from the many temples, and then, as if from nowhere, the haunting notes of a flute wandered above the moving crowd. It was all Mahesh could do to keep his mind upon the purpose of his journey. He pushed on to the massive, red walls of the Palace.

The palace gate was so vast and so ornate, Mahesh thought it must be the door to the Emperor's own home. But it was far from that. Beautiful as it was, it was merely the outermost edge of the great city within a city, which was the Imperial Court.

As soon as the guard on duty noticed the astonished gaze of this simple-looking country lad, he slashed the air with his spear and barred Mahesh's path.

"Where do you think you're going, oaf?"

"I have come to see the King," said Mahesh, mildly.

"Oh, have you?" sneered the guard. "Why, how very fortunate. His Majesty has been wondering when you'd come . . ."

"Yes, I know," said Mahesh. "Well, now I'm here."

"Fool!" snarled the guard. "Do you think Shah Akbar has time to waste with ignorant yokels? Go away!"

Mahesh looked at the quivering mustaches of this arrogant warrior and half smiled.

"Please, uncle. When you were younger, no doubt you fought wonderfully on the Emperor's frontiers. Now that they have given you this easy job—why do you want to risk it?"

The guard's jaw dropped.

"Why, you impudent worm! I'll lop off your head at a single . . . I'll . . . I'll . . ."

But he stopped short as Mahesh held out Akbar's ring. Even a guard could recognize the Imperial Seal.

"Many years ago," said Mahesh, "our good King sent for me. Now let me pass."

Annoyed, the guard saw he would have to admit the lad. But he was unwilling to let him go in for free.

"You can pass on one condition," he scowled. "If you obtain anything from the Emperor, you will give half to me."

"Agreed," smiled Mahesh, and entered.

Shade trees rocked with the breeze as Mahesh followed the path through the royal gardens. Cooling fountains murmured, and the perfume of roses coiled like an invisible serpent through the air.

Each building he passed seemed more magnificent than the last. Finally, he recognized that a pavilion of shimmering marble, with a forest of columns and fretted arches, must be the Hall of Public Audience. So many richly-dressed courtiers thronged there that he felt any one of them might turn out to be the King. But at last he saw, seated upon a throne of gold that was studded with flashing gems, a man of simple elegance, whose nobility glistened in his eyes. Mahesh knew. This was Akbar.

Sliding past Uzbek generals, Rajput princes, and Persian artists, Mahesh bowed before the Throne and said:

"May your shadow never grow less, O Full Moon!"

Akbar smiled.

"Ask a favor, O One of Bright Prospects."

"Your Majesty," said Mahesh, rising. "I have come at your command, which none dare disobey." And he handed the Emperor the ring which Akbar had given the country boy so many years ago.

The King laughed with pleasure.

"Welcome, welcome! What can I do for you? What can I give you? What is your heart's desire?"

The courtiers hushed at this unusually generous reception by the King. Who was this shabby-looking young man?

Mahesh thought for a moment and then said evenly:

"I would like you to punish me with one hundred lashes."

You could have heard a pin drop upon the gleaming marble floor.

"What!" exploded the king. "A hundred lashes? But you have done nothing wrong!"

"Will Your Majesty go back on his promise to fulfill my heart's desire?"

"Well, no . . . a King must always keep his word . . ."

So, with great reluctance, Akbar ordered Mahesh's back to be stripped. Then he commanded the Court Executioner to lay a hundred lashes of the whip across his nut-brown shoulders. To the acute interest of all the assembled courtiers, Mahesh endured every stroke with a stony expression and without uttering a sound.

But when the whip had cracked for the fiftieth time, Mahesh suddenly jumped up and shouted: "Stop!"

"Ah!" cried Akbar. "Then you see how foolish you are being . . ."

"No, Sire. It is only that when I came here to see you, I was unable to enter the Palace, unless I promised the guard at the front gate half of whatever the King's generosity would get me. So I have taken *my* half of the hundred lashes. Please be kind enough to deliver the *rest* of them to the guard."

The entire crowd shouted with laughter, and Akbar loudest of all. His fingers snapped, and in less time than it takes to tell, servants hauled the unhappy guard into the Presence Chamber to receive his humiliating "bribe."

When they dragged him out in disgrace, Akbar turned to Mahesh and said:

"You are as brave as when you were a child, and, if possible, you have grown even cleverer. I have tried in many ways to weed out corruption at my Court, but your little trick today will do more to make greedy officials honest than if I passed a thousand laws. From now on, since your wit is mightier than a warrior's sword, you shall be called '*Birbal.*' And you shall stay by my side and advise me in all things."

THE JUSTICE BELL

Shortly before Birbal's arrival, Akbar had moved his Court from Agra to the elegant new city of Fatehpur Sikri. He did this to be near the tomb of his mentor, Sheikh Salim Chishti, who had just died.

Akbar wanted to choose a new Judge for his new city, but without Sheikh Salim to advise him, the King's Council was taking some time to suggest a person suitably wise and honest for the post.

In the meantime, Akbar decided to hang a bell outside his private apartments in the Palace, with a rope dangling from his high verandah to the courtyard below. That way, if any citizen had been wronged, he could simply jingle the bell. Then the Emperor would lean out, hear the problem, and pass his judgment on the spot.

One day, at about noon, the bell sounded.

"What now?" growled Akbar, rising from the food which the harem servants had just placed in front of him.

But when he leaned out the window and looked below, there was no one to be seen.

"Must have been the wind," thought Akbar, returning to his table.

But no sooner had he seated himself than the bell jangled again.

"Just a minute," he said, jumping up. But, as before, there was not a soul to be seen near the bell rope so far below. The Emperor looked suspiciously at the bell, rang it once or twice, shrugged and started back to his lunch.

"If it is somebody's idea of a joke," he said darkly, "they will soon learn how hard it is to amuse a hungry king . . ."

But hardly had these words escaped his lips than the bell tingled again. Quick as a flash, the Emperor bounded to the balcony, just in time to see an old bullock, nothing but skin and bones, gnawing at the bell rope far below. Throwing his head back, Akbar laughed.

"Send Birbal to ask what the bullock wants," he commanded one of his servants. "After all, no subject shall ring the Justice Bell in vain!"

Birbal led the old animal to the stables and gave it hay. Then he made inquiries until its owner was found. He was a very old farmer with two sons. The next day, farmer, sons, and bullock were brought into the Imperial Presence.

"Is this your bullock?" asked Akbar.

"Yes, *Maharaj'*," stammered the old farmer.

"Why do you let it roam free near the Palace?"

"I did not know it would bother Your Majesty . . . but it is old and feeble, and we can no longer afford to feed it. So we have sent it away."

Now Birbal turned to the man's two sons:

"Does your father still work in the fields?"

"No," said one. "He is rather old for that these days."

"Then, Your Majesty, in accordance with the bullock's plea for justice by ringing the bell, I recommend that you send the bullock and the old farmer into exile together."

"So be it," said Akbar, smiling.

"But, Sire!" protested the old man. "How can I survive alone in the world at my time of life?"

"*Jahanpanah,'*" said the sons, "our father has worked hard in our fields all his life to give us a home. Please do not force us to abandon him in his old age."

Birbal said:

"Has not this bullock served you faithfully in the fields all its life? And do you not drive it away now that it is too weak and old to work?"

The three farmers hung their heads.

"It is your duty," pronounced the King, "to care for this faithful animal until its death."

The old man thought for a moment, and then promised:

"Yes, Sire. With all my heart."

BIRBAL THE JUDGE

The King's Council was still arguing about who should become the new Judge. Of course every counselor proposed one of his own relatives. That way he could count on a lenient sentence if ever he got in trouble—and considerable bribe money for influencing the sentences of others.

Akbar began to consider Birbal for the post. The King was convinced that he was intelligent enough; but there would be tremendous opposition among the nobles. Even the Queen was upset.

"How do you expect people to listen to this 'Birbal,' as you call him? Will a Prince of the Royal House accept the judgment of a poor Brahmin from a dirty village no one ever heard of?"

"They will accept what I command them to accept," said Akbar. "But don't you see how clever he is? I think he would make an excellent judge."

"Humph," sniffed the *Begum³* with her nose in the air. "If you are going to appoint a Hindu to an exalted position, I cannot understand why you pass over your own brother-in-law!"

Akbar winced.

"Your brother?" he asked lamely.

"What is wrong with my brother?" snapped the Queen. "Is he not a high-born Rajput Prince?"

"Jai Mal is a good warrior," said Akbar carefully.

"A superb warrior," corrected the Queen.

"Yes, of course," said Akbar. "But has he quite got that—that wisdom a judge requires?"

"Put him to the test," said the *Begum* proudly. "You will soon forget this 'Birbal' fellow you dragged in from a hunt, when you see the dazzling qualities your own brother-in-law possesses!"

Akbar smiled. The Queen was never more beautiful than when her anger gave luster to her Rajput pride.

The Emperor commanded Jai Mal and Birbal to appear before him. To the astonishment of his counselors, Akbar announced that one of them would become the new Judge of Fatehpur Sikri. To find out which one was better suited to the job, Akbar would present three cases to the two men. The one who solved the cases, or handed down the fairer sentence, would receive the judge's mantle.

Jai Mal smiled and turned his head slightly to the marble fretwork screen above the Audience Hall. Behind this, the Queen could watch all Court proceedings unseen. Her brother nodded as he caught her glistening eye—and without raising his head, Birbal noticed her, too.

THE FIRST CASE:
THE MANGO TREE

Two men came into the Imperial Presence: Shankar and Ramu. Both were small farmers.

"You have appealed for justice to the Crown," said Akbar gravely. "State your complaints."

Shankar spoke up fearlessly.

"*Maharaj*, there is a mango tree between our two farms and this man pretends that all the fruit is his, even though I have watered that tree since it was a sapling."

"How do you answer that?" Birbal asked the trembling old Ramu.

"Master," began Ramu in a frail thread of a voice. "I planted that tree on the day my first son was born. I have cared for it these thirty years. Now this man, Shankar, takes all the fruit he wants and even sells it."

Akbar rubbed his chin.

"Jai Mal, what is your verdict?"

Jai Mal was impatient with these farmers' affairs.

"These two men should be whipped and driven from the Court for wasting Your Majesty's precious time. There is no way to tell, from looking at a tree, who planted it. And, besides, how many mangoes can either of them eat?"

The courtiers joined Jai Mal in laughter. But Akbar did not laugh, and the merriment died suddenly on their lips.

"Birbal, what do you propose?"

"I would like to have the court adjourn," said Birbal quietly.

"What, more delay?" chided Jai Mal.

"So be it," commanded the Emperor, and the two farmers were sent home.

That night, Birbal disguised himself as a villager and made his way to Shankar's house. Pounding on the door, he cried out:

"Shankar! Shankar! Thieves are stealing your mangoes!"

It was late at night, and there was no answer. Birbal pounded the door again. At last, without even opening the door, Shankar's angry voice came from within:

"Go away, you fool! Do you think I am going to fight with thieves in the middle of the night over a few rotten mangoes? Let a man sleep in peace!"

Birbal smiled. Then he continued to the hut of Ramu. Knocking on his door he cried:

"Ramu! Ramu! Thieves are running away with the mangoes on the tree!"

"Eh?" shouted the old man inside. "Wife! Did you hear that? Get me my stick! Get me my knife! Now we have not only to defend our mango tree from that greedy neighbor, but from thieves as well! But I have planted it with my own hands, and it is almost like a child to me. Hurry, wife! My sandals!"

And so, not even seeing Birbal in the dark, Ramu ran off toward the mango tree.

Even when Ramu found no sign of thieves, Birbal saw that he climbed up into the tree and prepared to spend the whole night on a limb, guarding the fruit in case the thieves should return. Chuckling at Ramu's bravery, Birbal went home to his own, comfortable bed.

The next morning, an exhausted Ramu and a confident Shankar again presented themselves at Court.

"Well?" asked Akbar.

Birbal stepped forward.

"I have not been able to decide who owns the tree," he began.

The courtiers howled. Jai Mal smiled. And behind the marble screen the beautiful *Begum* rubbed her hands in glee.

Birbal held up his hand for silence.

"But here is what I propose. All the mangoes shall be gathered from the tree and divided equally between Ramu and Shankar. Then the tree itself shall be cut and splintered, and that, too, shall be divided between them, as firewood."

Jai Mal shot a black look at Birbal. Why hadn't he thought of that?

Shankar was the first to speak:

"You are wise and fair, Birbal *Sahib*.[4] I agree to this."

But Ramu was silent. Akbar leaned forward.

"Does this judgment please you, father?" asked the King.

"No, Sire," said Ramu. "I have tended that tree for over half my life. It has fed my family, shaded us after many a weary day's work in the fields, and given shelter to a thousand birds, who have brought music into our simple lives. I cannot see it cut down. Please, *Maharaj*, you may give my tree to Shankar."

You could have heard a cricket sing, for the entire Court now realized the truth. At last Birbal spoke:

"My sentence," he said, "is thirty lashes for Shankar, or let him pay thirty silver rupees to his honest neighbor, for it is to the Emperor himself that he has told this lie."

Akbar nodded and clapped his hands:

"Next case!"

THE SECOND CASE:
THE FALSE MOTHER

Now two women were led before the Throne, followed by a veiled maidservant of the palace, who held a child in her arms. Each woman claimed that the infant was her own. Each woman said that the other had stolen the baby from her. Both pleaded hysterically, shedding real tears and pulling their hair. It was hard to see which was lying.

Akbar turned to his brother-in-law:

"Jai Mal, how will you solve this case?"

Jai Mal thought a moment. Remembering the case of the mango tree, he decided to test the women in the same way.

"Have the child cut in two. Give half to each woman. That should end the quarrel."

But instead of behaving differently, as Jai Mal hoped, both women reacted exactly the same. Falling at the feet of the Emperor, they wailed for mercy. Their anguished sobs gave no clue as to which might be the real mother. Behind her screen the *Begum* bowed her head in shame.

Akbar turned to Birbal:

"Will you try this difficult case?"

Without a moment's hesitation, Birbal said:

"Let a servant bring a glass of poisoned buttermilk."

Both the hysterical women were stunned into silence. Only the cooing of the baby could be heard in the vaulted marble hall. Birbal whispered instructions to the servant.

When he came back with a jewel-encrusted cup, Birbal handed it to one of the women.

"Give this poison to the child," he ordered, "or you shall drink it yourself."

The woman froze in terror. She looked at the Emperor, but there was no sign that he would contradict Birbal's cruel command. Seeing no hope, she moved toward the maidservant holding the baby and murmured a prayer as she raised the glass to the infant's lips.

"No!" cried the other woman, and, darting forward, she snatched the cup, raised it to her own lips, and drained it to the last drop.

With a clang, the cup fell from her trembling hands to the marble floor. The court gasped as she sank to her knees, sobbing. The Emperor rose from his throne. But before he could reach the woman, Birbal was at her side, raising her up and saying:

"Only a true mother would make that sacrifice to save her child. There was no poison in the drink. Your baby is restored to you forever."

The courtiers roared their approval.

Jai Mal clenched his fists.

And Akbar clapped his hands:

"Next case!"

THE THIRD CASE:
THE SHAPE OF A DIAMOND

Two respectable merchants and four other men came before the Throne. Dhanlal was the first to speak:

"O Peacock of the Age, I am well known as a wealthy jeweler in the bazaar. Last night I invited this man, Prakash, to dine at my house. As he is also a jeweler and a member of my caste, I did not think he would steal from me. But in the presence of these four men, who were also my honored guests, he handled and admired a huge diamond which I recently purchased. This morning when I searched my house, the diamond was nowhere to be found. I am charging Prakash with theft."

"Just a moment," interrupted Jai Mal, hoping to get ahead of Birbal. "How do you know your other guests did not steal it?"

"Because," answered Dhanlal, "they are all honest men. They all agree to what they saw, while Prakash here will not admit that I even showed him a diamond."

"But he didn't!" shouted Prakash. "This man is a notorious cheat! He gets money from people by charging them with crimes they didn't commit. I never saw a diamond in his house, and these men didn't, either. They are just hired liars, that's all."

"Silence!" thundered Jai Mal. "You have no witnesses at all, so it is your word against five. I find you guilty."

"Birbal?" asked Akbar leaning back in his throne.

Birbal rubbed his chin a moment and then turned to the witnesses.

"All of you saw the diamond in Prakash's hand?"

"He was sitting at the table right next to me, drooling over it," said the first witness.

"He said it was one of the finest stones he had ever seen," said the second witness.

"He said it would fetch a fortune at the Palace," said the third witness.

"And he even said such a jewel could corrupt an honest man," added the last witness in triumph.

"But the point is, all four of you got a good look at the gem?" asked Birbal.

"Yes, yes," the witnesses said.

"Fine," said Birbal. "Each witness will now retire to a separate room."

When they were gone, Birbal had a servant bring four lumps of soft wax.

"Take these to the witnesses and tell each to mold the wax into the shape of the diamond they saw Prakash holding."

Dhanlal shifted nervously from one foot to the other, as the entire court waited for the witnesses to reappear.

When they returned the lumps of wax, Birbal examined them, smiled, and handed them to the King.

One was the shape of a square, one was a hexagon, one a triangle, and the last was oblong. Clearly there had been no diamond, so each so-called witness had made the shape according to his own fancy.

Akbar looked up in anger.

"Let the false witnesses be given thirty lashes each. Let Dhanlal be given fifty lashes, and let Prakash be given the finest jewel that Dhanlal owns! And beware, swindler," said the King to Dhanlal. "The next time you cheat it will cost you your life!"

The jewelers and the witnesses were led away.

Akbar turned to Jai Mal and said:

"Worthy brother-in-law, you come from a family of great soldiers. I hereby give you the command of 10,000 knights. But Birbal shall be the Judge of Fatehpur Sikri."

Jai Mal was not satisfied, however, and to Akbar's great displeasure, he did not offer humble thanks but said:

"Your Majesty's wisdom is the finest pearl in the necklace of India's blessings. But I do not think this Birbal, who has only proved his mind runs along the same lines as farmers, quarreling housewives, and petty tricksters, should be exalted to the high rank of Judge. After all, a judge deals with matters of state and the dignity of the Crown. Surely a judge should be a man of noble birth."

Behind the screen of marble the *Begum* swelled with pride at her brother's clever words. Akbar stared for a moment at his brother-in-law with dislike. Then he said:

"If you will abide by the results of one more test, I shall consider your point."

This time Jai Mal bowed with great humility.

"Hearing is obedience, *Jahanpanah*."

"Very well," said Akbar. "I shall submit another case to the two candidates at this hour tomorrow morning."

And the courtiers all bowed as the Emperor left the Hall of Public Audience.

THE FOURTH CASE:
THE KING'S MUSTACHE

At breakfast the next morning, Akbar still had not decided what test of wit he would give the two candidates. Suddenly his young son, Prince Sultan Salim, jumped up on his lap and playfully pulled his father's mustache. Not only did it hurt, but Akbar was sharply annoyed at having his thoughts disturbed.

"Get down!" shouted Akbar. "Why, do you know that anyone else, from the mountains of Kashmir to the shores of Bengal, could be put to death for pulling the Emperor's mustache?"

Prince Salim slunk down off the couch, crestfallen. But hardly had these words left his lips than Akbar smiled. Rising and wrapping his turban, he strode off to the Hall of Public Audience.

When Jai Mal and Birbal made their obeisance before the Throne, Akbar said:

"You have asked to try a case involving the dignity of the Crown. Very well. It will shock you to learn that this very morning somebody came into my presence and insulted your Emperor by actually pulling his mustache—"

The entire Court gasped.

Akbar held up his hand.

"Yes, I know. So I ask the distinguished candidates: what punishment fits this crime?"

Jai Mal stepped forward.

"Your Majesty, my father was a King, though he hardly approached the exalted excellence of your own glorious Presence. Nevertheless, the King's Person is sacred to the people. To insult the King is to insult our

Motherland. Therefore, this rude person has committed treason against the state, and he should die."

Everyone nodded in agreement. Except Birbal.

"Does the other candidate agree?" asked the Emperor.

"*Maharaj*," said Birbal, smiling. "I would suggest that this 'culprit' be adorned with golden wristlets and receive sweets from the Emperor's own hand."

The courtiers and even the Queen behind her marble screen were puzzled. Jai Mal was aghast.

"Have you gone mad?" he gobbled at Birbal

But Akbar laughed out loud.

"Why do you recommend this sentence, Birbal?"

"Because, *Huzur*[5], I can hardly believe, in this well-guarded palace in the mightiest city on earth, that anyone could possibly have pulled the Imperial Mustache except your own little son, and Jai Mal's nephew, Prince Sultan Salim."

"Approach the Throne!" thundered the Great Mughal, rising. And turning to the assembled Court he said:

"Know that this man is appointed to the high rank of Judge of Fatehpur Sikri. His wise decisions shall be respected by all as the will of the Crown. And he shall be known from this day forward as Wazir Birbal—Minister to the King!"

THE QUEEN'S PLOT

The Queen and her brother Jai Mal were very bitter about Birbal's appointment as Judge. Jai Mal snarled:

"If Birbal had not been in my way, the appointment would have been mine for the taking."

"Your problem, brother," said the Queen, "is that you spend all your time hunting and trying on clothes. The Emperor has no faith in you."

"The Emperor loves hunting as much as I do," growled Jai Mal. "The problem is, this upstart has convinced Akbar that nobody can outsmart him. Now if only we could trap Birbal . . ."

"Ah," said the *Begum*, flashing a beautiful smile. "You and the Emperor may hunt tigers, but I will teach you the art of trapping men . . ."

That evening when the Emperor entered his private apartments, the Queen began pouting, staring into the distance, and sighing repeatedly. At length Akbar looked up from a map of Gujarat which he had been studying and asked:

"How long are you going to be upset about your worthless brother not getting a job he doesn't deserve, Salima?"

The Queen's eyes snapped with fury.

"And who does deserve it—that son of village woodcutters? He has won over your mind, but Birbal is not half so clever as you think."

"Well," said the King, "even if I wanted to get rid of Birbal, I've already given him the appointment. I can hardly take it back for no reason."

"I can give you a reason."

"Really?" said Akbar. "What?"

"Give him some task to perform," said the Queen. "He is bound to fail. Then you can dismiss him for incompetence."

The King chuckled.

"Very well, Incomparable Pearl. You suggest the task."

Delighted, the Queen clutched Akbar's arm and whispered into his ear:

"When you are in the palace garden tomorrow, insist that Birbal bring me to you. He will not succeed, come what may."

Akbar agreed and laid her beautiful head upon his shoulder. The Queen smiled and thought:

"It is in my power now, Birbal, to see you fall . . ."

Next morning, as birds murmured thoughtfully in the trees, Birbal chanced upon Akbar, looking very downcast in the rose garden.

"The cares of a King are written upon your brow, Great Presence."

"Birbal," answered Akbar, "it is the Empress. We have quarreled, and now she refuses to see me. But you could persuade her if anyone can. Go and bring her to me at once."

"Hearing is obedience, *Maharaj.*"

"But if you fail," added Akbar, doing his best to smuggle a smile, "you will lose your position as Judge, and I will give it instead to the *Begum*'s brother, Jai Mal."

"I understand you, *Jahanpanah*," said Birbal, now also suppressing a smile.

He went without delay to the Queen's palace. At the gate, Birbal pulled a servant aside and commanded him:

"In five minutes come to me in the Queen's apartments. Give me this exact message—"

And Birbal told the servant what to say.

With his eyes respectfully on the floor, Birbal was ushered into the presence of the proud and lovely Queen.

"*Begum Sahiba⁶*," he began, "I bring you a message from His Majesty. He awaits you in the palace garden, and—"

But at that moment the obedient servant came up next to Birbal and tugged his sleeve.

"What is it?" asked Birbal, annoyed.

The servant shot a nervous look at the Queen.

"This is for your ears only, sir," mumbled the servant.

"Excuse me a moment, Your Highness," said Birbal, withdrawing politely—but not quite out of earshot—from the Queen.

Curious as she was beautiful, the *Begum* crept up to the curtain which separated her from Birbal and heard the servant whisper these words:

"She—is—*beautiful* . . ."

The Queen stood up in shock. Birbal nodded, dismissed the servant, and returned to the Queen. He was grinning impudently as he told her:

"The situation has changed completely, *Begum Sahiba*. The King no longer needs you to come."

And Birbal slipped away, leaving the Queen afire with suspicion.

"Did I not hear the servant say something about a beautiful maiden?" she thought. "Is it possible the Emperor does not want me to see her with him?"

Unable to control her jealousy, the Queen ran from her palace and down the garden path. There she found Akbar alone. He looked up from smelling a rose.

"My dear wife!" he laughed. "You promised you would not come."

Stamping her foot, the Queen complained:

"I have been tricked into coming by your Minister, Birbal!"

"Tricked?" asked the King grinning. "If he told you a lie, I shall have him severely punished."

The *Begum* bit her lip.

"How can I tell him that fear of a beautiful rival brought me running?" she thought.

Out loud she said:

"No. All he told me was that the situation had changed."

Akbar roared laughing.

"That's all? You came because he only told you that?"

"I shall never forgive you," she snapped.

But Akbar put his strong arm around the Queen's slender shoulders, laid her head upon his chest, and said:

"You have too kind a heart not to forgive me, Incomparable Pearl. And one day you will also forgive Wazir Birbal. Now, come, let us go to the reflecting pool and view the water lilies which have bloomed this morning . . ."

BIRBAL AND THE
PAMPERED QUEEN

It was not long before those words about forgiveness were proven true. One day Akbar took Birbal with him on a walk. Outside the Palace, they passed some women who had been pressed into hard labor.

They were repairing the road, shoveling and breaking up solid rock. The Great Mughal was shocked at the difference between the hard life of these poor women and the luxury of his pampered Queen.

As soon as he got back to the palace, he gave an unheard-of order. From that day forward, the Queen would perform all the household tasks with her own hands.

"If women in the villages can work so hard when they are half starved," said Akbar, "there is no reason why women in my palace should lie about. It is ridiculous not to be able to dress yourself or comb your own hair. They have been spoiled."

Now the Empress was a high-born noblewoman, used to milk baths and rare fragrances. She had always been surrounded by a dozen ladies-in-waiting. The sudden change from life in a cushioned harem to seamstress, cook, and washerwoman was too much for her delicate nature. Under the strain, she lost seven pounds in a week and never felt so wretched in her life.

When Birbal came to pay Her Majesty respects, he found her in an alarming state. But he tried to conceal his surprise.

"O Birbal," sobbed the Queen, "you are just the man I am looking for. Surely you can help me if anyone can. If I go on much longer like this, I am sure to die."

When Birbal heard the story of Akbar's strange command, he smiled, pondered, and then said:

"Give me five days, and I think I will make the King see the error of his ways."

"Five days!" cried the *Begum*. "You shall have my gratitude for five decades, if only you can move the King."

At the end of five days, Akbar decided to stroll through his garden of exotic plants. This park was a botanical library, growing the rarest and most beautiful flora in the world. They were in the care of a highly talented gardener. So the Emperor was furious to find his prize plants all yellow and withered in the merciless Indian sun.

"Gardener!" he bellowed. "What have you done? What is the meaning of this neglect?"

"*Jahanpanah*," said the terrified gardener, "it is on Birbal's orders. I have not watered them for a week."

When Birbal was summoned before the Great Mughal, he was all sweetness and smiles.

"By Heaven, Birbal, what idiotic order have you given?"

"Idiotic, Majesty? But I was just reflecting. The great banyan trees grow strong and tall in the forest; yet we never water them. Why should these lazy garden plants have special treatment?"

"Fool!" thundered the King. "Anyone knows the most exotic plants are also the most frail."

But even as he spoke, Akbar remembered the harsh orders he had given his delicate Queen.

Akbar and Birbal traded a knowing smile.

And the ladies-in-waiting were again drawing the *Begum*'s bath of fragrant milk that afternoon.

GALLOWS OF GOLD

So the Queen was reconciled to Wazir Birbal. But her brother, Jai Mal, was certainly not. Jai Mal even sent a secret letter to King Abdullah of Uzbekistan, offering to help raise the banner of revolt against the Mughal Crown. But spies intercepted the letter and sent it to Akbar. He was furious.

"This only proves," the King roared, "that nothing good can come from brothers-in-law. Let every brother-in-law in my Empire be hung!"

The court was shocked. Many noblemen protested, but the King would not listen.

"Carry out my orders," he fumed.

The courtiers were at a complete loss. Nobody wanted to be associated with an order which would earn the hatred of all the people. Then someone suggested:

"Let Birbal do it."

And, to everyone's surprise, Birbal readily agreed.

First, he went to Jai Mal.

"You may hate me, but know that the King read your letter to King Abdullah."

Jai Mal turned sickly white.

"This order against brothers-in-law is aimed at you," said Birbal.

"What can I do?" gasped Jai Mal.

"Will you give up plotting and promise lifelong loyalty to the King?"

"I will promise anything," stammered the terrified Prince.

"Well, let us see," said Birbal, and he went off to supervise the building of the gallows.

All over Fatehpur Sikri the dismal sound of hammering marked the final hour for thousands of innocent men. Gallows sprung up like weeds around the capital. On the fourth day, Birbal led the Emperor out on a balcony to view the forest of grisly gibbets.

"I thought you should see the preparations, *Jahanpanah*. Everything is almost ready."

The King surveyed the bristling execution ground with satisfaction. Then a brilliant flash in the morning sun caught his eye, and he peered carefully in its direction, shading his brow. Side by side stood two magnificently fashioned gallows, one of silver and another of gold.

"What sort of wasteful expenditure is that?" asked the King. "Who asked you to make gallows of silver and gold?"

"It seemed only fitting," murmured Birbal somberly.

"Fitting?" asked Akbar, exasperated. "We are only hanging brothers-in-law here. For whom are these special gallows made?"

"The silver one," said Birbal, "is for my insignificant self, while the golden one is for you, O Axis of the Earth."

"For me?" exclaimed the Emperor. "Who dares to send me to the gallows?"

"You go upon your own orders, *Maharaj*. For if Jai Mal is brother-in-law to you, you also are brother-in-law to him. Tomorrow, as the most distinguished of brothers-in-law, you must hang first, to be followed by this brother-in-law, and just about everybody else."

The Emperor kicked a pebble with his foot.

"Oh, very well," he grumbled. "Call the whole thing off."

And all the gallows in the land were put to the flame.

Jai Mal kept his pledge of loyalty to Akbar—but he had promised Birbal nothing, and he continued to plot against him.

THE SOUP OF THE DUCK

When Birbal had secured his fortune at court, the first person he thought of was his mother. He returned to his native village, Tikawanpur, on the banks of the river Jumna, and brought her back to Fatehpur Sikri in a splendid caravan, along with her entire household. He gave her a luxurious apartment in his shimmering palace and provided every comfort and pleasure his mother could desire.

Birbal's mother was wonderfully proud of her clever and generous son. As soon as she got over the surprise of so many incredible dreams coming true, she began sending a stream of joyful letters to her relatives back in the village. The people of Tikawanpur could hardly believe her stories of life in the elegant court of Shah Akbar.

Before long, some of Birbal's poor relations began to ask themselves, "Why should we not share some of the glory that our cousin Birbal has earned?"

So one of Birbal's cousins decided to make the journey to the fabled city of Fatehpur Sikri to seek out Birbal's fortune.

"I should not go empty-handed," thought the cousin. So he chose the fattest duckling from the animals on his farm and went his way.

When he entered the gates of Fatehpur Sikri, he was just as astonished as Birbal had been when he had made his first journey there as Mahesh Das. The country cousin was even more amazed at Birbal's fame—everyone in the bazaar knew how to direct him to Birbal's house. And what a house! It was a palace of towering red sandstone with courtly gardens and laughing fountains. No one in Tikawanpur had ever dreamed of such a home.

Timidly, the cousin made his way through fretted columns to the *diwan*[7]. A servant on whispering feet went to announce his arrival to Birbal.

In mere moments, Birbal appeared, dressed in gorgeous garments of silk and gold.

"Welcome! Welcome!" he laughed. "Since you are from my village of Tikawanpur, you are my brother. But please, friend, let me know your name."

"I . . . I am your cousin," stammered the villager. "And I have brought you this . . . this duck."

"Splendid!" cried Birbal. "Then we shall have him roasted for lunch."

Birbal clapped his hands, and servants appeared as if from nowhere. They took the duck to the kitchen and the country cousin to a magnificent chamber, where he had a hot bath and dressed in new and costly robes. When he had rested, the servants brought him to the banquet hall. There he sat down with Birbal to a feast of a hundred exquisite dishes. In the center of the table was a crisp, magnificent, roast duck.

"Now tell me the news of Tikawanpur," smiled Birbal. And the cousins enjoyed a happy afternoon together.

The next day, Birbal loaded his cousin with princely gifts and sent him on his way.

Back in Tikawanpur, the villagers were dazzled with the tales of Birbal's wealth and position of honor.

"Everyone in the capital speaks of him as if he were the Emperor himself," declared the cousin. "They say he is the Emperor's best friend, and the splendor of his surroundings proves it!"

"Then everything his mother wrote was true," cried the villagers. And all of Birbal's other cousins decided to make a journey to the city to claim their share of Birbal's wealth.

The next week, another of Birbal's distant relatives walked the long road to Fatehpur Sikri. While he was waiting to be announced at Birbal's house, he suddenly remembered that he had forgotten to bring a gift. When Birbal appeared, thinking quickly, he stammered,

"I am a cousin of the cousin who brought you the duck."

Smiling, Birbal said, "Welcome, brother." And he dressed the villager in gorgeous robes, treated him to a banquet of a hundred dishes, and sent him home laden with precious gifts.

The next week, another villager from Tikawanpur appeared at Birbal's house and said,

"I am a cousin of the cousin of the cousin who brought you the duck."

Smiling, Birbal again gave the man rich garments to wear, presented a sumptuous feast, and sent him home with costly gifts.

The next week, another villager from Tikawanpur arrived and said,

"I am a cousin of the cousin of the cousin of the cousin who brought you the duck."

This time Birbal smiled a little less, but he invited the man in, gave him luxurious robes, feasted him, and sent him home with gifts.

The next week, another villager from Tikawanpur arrived and told Birbal,

"I am a cousin of the cousin of the cousin of the cousin of the cousin who brought you the duck."

At last Birbal was tired of feasting his lazy cousins from Tikawanpur who all wanted something for nothing. So he invited the villager in, gave him beautiful robes to wear, and then went to the kitchen and told his cook, "Boil some water."

When the water was hot, he said,

"Pour the hot water into two soup bowls and bring them for our lunch."

Birbal sat down with his country cousin, smiled, and, when the hot water was placed before them, he said, with a magnificent gesture,

"Eat in good health!"

The villager stared blankly at the water in the saucer. Then he sipped it. He tasted nothing.

"What is this?" he asked.

"Ah," grinned Birbal, "that is the soup of the soup of the soup of the soup of the soup of the duck that your cousin brought."

And after spooning all the water down with great relish, Birbal sent his cousin back to the village empty-handed.

From that day forward, Birbal had no more visitors from Tikawanpur.

THE FIRST PRIZE

Mir Sayyid Ali and Abud-us Samad were two of Persia's greatest masters of painting. They entered the Emperor Humayun's service when he was a refugee at Shah Tahmasp's Court, and they created a flourishing studio under Akbar.

Certain people—and Shah Tahmasp was one of them—thought painting was frivolous. But Akbar said: "Such men I dislike."

The Mughal Emperor examined the work of his Court painters every week, judged their merit, and rewarded them well.

One day the son of a poor coachman presented himself at Court, claiming to have artistic gifts.

"If Your Majesty permits, I want to arrange an exhibition of my pictures in the courtyard of your Palace."

"Willingly," smiled the King. "But to make things more interesting, instead of a mere show, let it be a competition. You, Ali, and Samad will each exhibit your best work. The people of Sikri will judge whose is finest."

On the appointed day, the two great masters and the son of the poor coachman brought their canvases to the King.

Mir Sayyid Ali had painted a picture of rare and delicate blossoms. They looked so real that bees and wasps buzzed around them—so persistently that the guards could not shoo them away. The people murmured at the talent of this wonderful man.

Abud-us Samad had painted a picture of a rolling meadow, lush and covered with dew. A passing cow walked straight to the canvas and attempted to nibble the tender shoots. There was a hum of admiration as, with difficulty, the guards led the wistful animal aside.

Now, the third canvas, which had been painted by the poor coachman's son, was still veiled.

"Uncover it, Birbal," said the King, "and let us see if the boy has promise."

So Birbal reached for the curtain—but instantly pulled back his hand in shock. His fingertips were wet with paint! Then he realized that the subject of this picture was—simply a curtain.

"Bees and cows may be duped by anyone," laughed Akbar, "but to fool a clever man like Birbal is a great victory for any artist. This achievement easily wins the prize."

And so the poor coachman's lad, whose name was Daswant, attained the exalted name of "First Master of the Age"—another Jewel in the Mughal Crown.

THE PATRON OF THE ARTS

Many of the courtiers imitated the Emperor, commissioning paintings from his artists. But one nobleman, Munim Khan, had no wish to waste money on scribbling fools.

One day in *durbar*[8], the Emperor said, "Munim Khan has proven a loyal subject. But I do not think a nobleman is truly noble if he shows no interest in art."

Taking the hint, Munim Khan sent for Daswant, who dutifully came to the Khan's beautiful home.

"I don't see the point of it, but just to please the Emperor, I want to commission a painting from you. They say you have talent."

Daswant bowed low and humbly murmured, "Your praise is too kind, *Huzur*."

"Probably it is," frowned Munim Khan. "But let's see how good you are. How much will it cost to have you paint my portrait?"

"The usual fee is one hundred silver rupees, sir," said Daswant.

Munim Khan choked. "A hundred silver rupees! That's robbery!"

"That is the usual fee," said Daswant firmly.

"Very well," scowled the Khan. "You shall have your fee, but I warn you, the painting must be an exact likeness of me. If not, you shall not have even a copper *paisa*."

"Hearing is obedience, O Munificent One," smiled Daswant. And he went to work, making studies and sketches of Munim Khan's head. At the end of the day, he went back to his studio to finish the portrait.

After a week's hard work, Daswant returned to the home of Munim Khan, proudly bearing a beautiful portrait, trimmed in paint of silver and gold.

But Munim Khan scowled and said, "This doesn't look anything like me. Look here, you have painted me with a beard."

Daswant was astonished. He looked and, indeed, Munim Khan had shaved off his beard! Only his long mustache was left.

"But, sir, you had a beard when I painted you," said Daswant.

"I said a perfect likeness, and this does not look like me. Do it right, or you shall not be paid."

So Daswant took out his pencils and paper and made new sketches of Munim Khan wearing only his mustache. Then he went back to his studio, and, after a week of tireless work, brought back a lovely new portrait in ruby and sapphire hues.

But Daswant halted in his tracks when he saw the Khan—now he had shaved off his mustache, too!

Munim Khan picked up the portrait, shook his head, and said, "No. As you can see, it looks nothing like me. This fellow has a mustache. I do not. Try again."

Sadly, Daswant made sketches of the clean-shaven Munim Khan, went back to work, and returned in one week with a new masterpiece.

"What will it be now?" Daswant wondered. He soon found out. The Khan reappeared with his beard and mustache all grown back.

"This is not an exact likeness," said Munim Khan, frowning at the clean-shaven portrait. "If you can show me an exact likeness of myself, you shall have a hundred silver rupees. If not, you shall have nothing. And to think" he sneered, "they call you 'First Master of the Age' . . ."

A miserable Daswant headed homeward through the streets of Fatehpur Sikri. On the way, he ran into Birbal.

"Why so down?" smiled Birbal. "Have you run out of subjects to paint?"

"Run out!" cried Daswant. "I just wish I could pin one down!" And he explained his problem.

Birbal laughed.

"Come to *durbar* tomorrow," he told Daswant. "With the Emperor's help, we will set everything right."

Munim Khan was in the Hall of Public Audience early the next day. When Akbar had finished the serious business of state, he asked if any of his ministers had further matters.

Birbal stepped forward.

"Sire," he said, "I have heard that Munim Khan offers one hundred silver rupees to the artist who will show him an exact likeness of himself."

Akbar was pleased. "Is this true?" he asked the Khan.

"Yes, Your Majesty," murmured Munim Khan, looking darkly at Birbal.

"I also have heard that Daswant himself has failed three times to pass the test," Birbal said

Akbar was astonished. "My most talented artist?" he cried.

Daswant bowed his head. "Yes, Sire, it is true. Munim Khan is a very difficult subject to paint."

"Well, Sire," said Birbal, "I would like to earn the 100 silver rupees myself."

"You, Birbal?" grinned Akbar. "You can't even draw a straight line! How can you succeed where Daswant has failed?"

"Does Munim Khan agree that he will pay 100 silver rupees to any artist who can show him an exact likeness of himself?"

"By the beard of the Prophet," swore Munim Khan.

"Well, then, here you are." And Birbal handed Munim Khan a small mirror.

Munim Khan grew red-faced. "How dare you play games with me?" he shouted. "This is no portrait, it's, it's—"

"It's an exact likeness of yourself." smiled Birbal.

"You swore by the beard of the Prophet!" laughed the Emperor.

"Bah," growled Munim Khan. "You are some artist, Birbal!" And he threw Birbal the hundred silver coins.

"And you, Munim Khan *Sahib*" replied Birbal, tossing the bag of coins to Daswant, "are now a patron of the arts!"

FATE

One day Akbar and Birbal went hunting with a huge and colorful entourage. After several hot hours of hard riding, the two got separated from the other sportsmen in a dense jungle. Akbar was furious.

"Look, I'm King," he grumbled to Birbal. "How is it possible to be surrounded by courtiers stupid enough to actually lose me?"

But Birbal was calm.

"Everything is a matter of Fate, Your Majesty. Good may come of it," he said.

Akbar was annoyed, but he said nothing as they rode in search of water. Finally he burst out:

"My Empire contains a thousand mighty rivers, and I can't even find a glass of water to slake my thirst!"

"It may work out for the best," remarked Birbal.

These words had hardly left his lips when the two broke into a clearing with a small well. Akbar reined in his horse.

"At last! Birbal, dismount and fetch me a drink."

"Hearing is obedience, Sire." And, so saying, Birbal slipped from his saddle and headed for the well.

As Akbar began to dismount, however, his finger snagged one of the glistening arrows in his quiver, and the King cried out in pain.

"Now look what's happened!" he shouted, trying to stop the flow of blood. "My fat doctor is probably gobbling a hot lunch in camp while I bleed! Could anything else possibly go wrong?"

"Everything happens for the best," murmured Birbal, raising water from the well.

But Akbar had heard this one time too many.

"How dare you say such stupid, shallow things when I'm in pain?" bellowed the King. And, in a fit of anger, he flung Birbal down the well.

The gratifying splash made Akbar feel immediately better. But he had hardly started to peer over the edge of the well, when he felt the unmistakable prickling of eyes upon his back.

Wheeling around, he discovered to his horror that he was surrounded by half-naked tribals, all of whom had their poisoned arrows trained upon his heart. Getting a grip on himself, he drew up to his full height and announced:

"I am Shah Akbar of Hindustan. Kneel before your Emperor."

But the tribals only rattled their bows threateningly. One of them stepped forward, croaking:

"Whoever you may be, I am Todar, chief of the cannibals in these parts. We are going to sacrifice you to the Death Goddess, Durgha!"

"Help, Birbal!" wailed the King. But the black depths of the well returned no sound.

The cannibals dragged the helpless Mughal and bound him to the altar of their goddess. But just as everything was ready for the sacrifice, one of the tribals noticed blood still dripping from Akbar's finger.

"Stop!" he cried out. The cannibal chief saw the bleeding finger, and he spat angrily on the grass.

"What bad luck," said Todar. "Everyone knows you cannot offer a sacrifice to the goddess if it is imperfect. That cut finger has saved this fellow's life. Too bad. He looks like he would have been a tasty one."

Intensely relieved and rewinding his trampled turban, the Great Mughal limped back to the clearing and bashfully hallooed for Birbal down the well. This time there was an answer.

"I'm so sorry," said the King, as he guiltily hauled Birbal up. "You were quite right. Everything does happen for the best."

"Yes, *Maharaj*," said Birbal.

But as Birbal was wringing the water from his clothes, the King suddenly had a thought.

"Just tell me this," said Akbar mischievously to his sodden friend. "Though my cut finger did save me, what benefit did you get from my throwing you down a well?"

Birbal grinned.

"Since my finger was *not* cut, being down a well was the only thing that saved me from being sacrificed in your place! That every adversity contains the seed of a greater benefit, *Jahanpanah*, is what I call—fate."

THE DONKEY'S HAIRCUT

T he court barber was an arrogant fellow. He had served both Akbar's father and his grandfather. He considered himself almost part of the dynasty. As such, he also trimmed the beards of some of the wealthiest and most cultured men in Fatehpur Sikri. This lofty company made the barber feel greedy and somewhat above the law.

One day, a poor old woodcutter trudged into the city market after a long morning in the mountains splitting logs and tying them into bundles. His broken-down old donkey—a companion of fifteen years—swayed under his burden of firewood.

As the woodcutter plodded past the barber's shop, calling his wares, the barber poked his head through the curtains and yelled:

"How much for everything on that donkey?"

"Five copper *paisa*, sir," said the woodcutter.

"I'll give you four," sniffed the barber, counting the coins down on the bench before him.

The old woodcutter shrugged and said:

"Mine is a fair price, but these are hard times."

So he off-loaded his bundles, took the money, and led his donkey on the homeward path.

But he had hardly gone half a mile when he remembered that his ax had been tied up in the bundles of firewood, and he would need it for the next morning's work.

Running back to the barber shop, he panted:

"*Huzur*, I would not have bothered you, but those bundles I sold you— my ax is tied up in one of them, and I shall need it for tomorrow. I go to the hills to chop firewood two hours before dawn . . ."

But the barber was busy with a wealthy caravan merchant and growled: "Go away."

"But, sir, my ax—it is more precious than diamonds to me, sir. I cannot support my family without it, and I certainly cannot afford to buy another—"

"I told you to be gone!" shouted the barber. "You sold me everything on your donkey for four copper *paisa*, and if your ax was bound up with the load, so much the worse for you. Now go, before I call the city guards!"

Miserable, the woodcutter staggered away. He was faced with complete ruin, and he did not know what to do. Then, for some reason, he thought of the new Judge, Birbal, whom all the people had been gossiping about. He asked a spice merchant for directions and headed immediately to Birbal's house.

"We can take the matter before the King," mused Birbal, "but I think, in the case of this rich and influential barber, he will win. After all, you admit you did agree to sell him everything on your donkey . . ."

"But what can I do?" wailed the woodcutter. "Without the ax, my family will starve!"

"Listen to me," said Birbal sharply, and the woodcutter closed his mouth. "Here is what you will do . . ."

And on Birbal's instructions, the woodcutter went the next morning to the barber's stall and said:

"Friend barber, I apologize for making that scene yesterday. After thinking about it, I realized you were right. Will you please let bygones be bygones?"

"Humph," said the barber. "Why not?"

"Oh, thank you," smiled the woodcutter. "Then will you also let me know what you will charge to shave myself and a companion?"

The barber looked at the woodcutter with dislike. He was not used to such shabby customers. But the barber had a policy—never say no, just name a higher price.

"Twenty silver rupees," he snapped. To his amazement, the woodcutter agreed, immediately counting the coins down on the barber's bench.

Shrugging, the barber put them in his money box and shaved the woodcutter. When he had finished, he asked:

"Now where's your companion?"

"There," said the woodcutter, pointing to his donkey.

"A donkey!" shouted the barber. "Why you stupid, impudent oaf! Get out of here and never show your face at my shop again!"

But at that moment Birbal wandered by and heard the explanations of both men.

"This is a difficult case," said the Judge. "I would like to put it to the King."

So there were many curious spectators when the barber and the woodcutter brought their complaints before the Throne.

When Akbar had heard the matter of the ax, he turned to the woodcutter sorrowfully and said:

"I am sorry for you, my son, but a deal is a deal. If the barber were generous, he would not hesitate to return your ax. But I am afraid I cannot force him to do this."

But when the case went on, and Akbar heard the story of the donkey, he burst out laughing:

"I suspect you have had a very good advisor, woodcutter, and all I can say is: a deal is a deal! Barber, you will have to honor your side."

So the miserable barber was forced to soap down the donkey and shave him bald as a pomegranate, ruining seven good razors. All the while, dozens of chuckling noblemen and shopkeepers looked on.

"A little more off the top!" called one.

"Don't nick him, or we'll demand a refund!" cried another.

"Don't stint on the aftershave!" shouted a third. And the crowd rippled with laughter.

No sooner had the woodcutter begun to lead his perfumed and chilly donkey away, than another wag led a camel to the barber shop and loudly asked:

"How much to shave a little off the hump?"

Surrounded by giggles and jeers from the entire bazaar, the barber grabbed the woodcutter's ax, and ran, red-faced, after him.

"Here!" he screamed, thrusting it into the old man's hands. "Take your cursed ax and never darken my doorstep again! And the rest of you buffoons," he called to the crowd, "why don't you find something useful to do?"

The barber stormed back to his shop and snapped its curtains shut behind him.

And from that day forward, he nursed a bitter grudge against Wazir Birbal.

BIRBAL AND THE PERSIAN SHAH

Before Akbar was born, his father, the Emperor Humayun, had lost his throne. He, his Queen, and a few loyal friends fled to Persia to escape their enemies and accept the protection of that munificent monarch, Shah Tahmasp.

Before they reached the territory of Persia, Akbar was born at Amerkot, on October 15, 1542. When Humayun saw his newborn son, he handed a piece of fragrant musk to each in his small circle of friends and said:

"May the fame of my son fill the world, as this musk perfumes the air. I shall call him Akbar, which means Most Great."

Akbar did, of course, become a very great king, but Shah Abbas of Persia never let him forget the favors his predecessor had done Humayun and the Mughal family. He always addressed the Mughal Emperor as "Younger Brother" in his letters and found a hundred other ways to imply that Akbar's glittering fame was all because of the generous Persian Shah.

"It is said," Akbar commented one day, "that whoever receives a favor should never forget it. But whoever does a favor should never mention it. I wonder if this proverb is current in Persia . . ."

Still, Akbar let the matter go. Then one day, the Shah began to think of waging war on India and adding Akbar's Empire to his own. Yet travelers told so many marvels of the Mughal Court, Shah Abbas thought it would be wise to know more about India before trying to invade. The Shah asked Akbar to send him an ambassador who could inform him of the wonders of Hindustan.

Akbar wanted to impress the Shah once and for all, so he selected Birbal as his emissary, loading him down with treasures of India as gifts for the Persian King.

When Birbal reached Ispahan, he was conducted with music and pomp into the Presence Chamber, as befitted an envoy of the Great Mughal.

But Birbal's gaze fell upon a most astonishing sight: instead of one throne, there were twelve—and upon them, twelve identical Shahs!

"It is a test," thought Birbal. "Yet I must quickly decide which is the true Shah and bow to him, or he will be offended."

Letting his eyes travel down the row of thrones, Birbal suddenly smiled, knelt respectfully before one of the shahs, and said:

"My lord and master, Akbar, Emperor of India, conveys his felicitations and respects to the exalted Shahinshah[10] of Persia."

"Wazir Birbal," laughed the Shahinshah. "You have never seen me before. How did you recognize me?"

"Your Majesty," said Birbal. "As I stood perplexed, I noticed that all the other 'shahs' looked at *you* for *your* reaction, while you alone fixed your gaze on *me*."

Marveling at Birbal's keen sense of observation, the Shah replied:

"Truly you are an ocean of intelligence, Wazir Birbal. But tell me, now that you have traversed many kingdoms on your journey here, what can you say about me in comparison with other kings?"

"Your Majesty is the Full Moon, while the other kings are only glowworms."

The King of Persia smiled.

"And how do I compare with my younger brother, Akbar of Hindustan?" he asked.

Birbal answered promptly:

"The Emperor Akbar is the New Moon."

The Shah was delighted and loaded Birbal with gifts for his return home.

But news of Birbal's beautiful compliment to the Persian King reached India before him, and Akbar was very angry. He brushed the gifts from Ispahan aside and thundered:

"Birbal, you have betrayed and insulted me! How dare you call the Persian Shah the Full Moon, while comparing me to nothing but a crescent?"

"*Jahanpanah*," replied Birbal, "the Full Moon grows smaller day by day, while the New Moon has all its glory before it."

Akbar laughed and embraced his friend, while the spies in Fatehpur Sikri swiftly conveyed this conversation back to the Shah.

"The wisdom of Akbar's advisors," said Shah Abbas, "makes our sages seem like fools."

And never again did he contemplate war against the mighty ruler of Hindustan.

CATS

One day in the King's Council, Akbar proposed a war against Burma. He asked his nobles: "What do you think?"

"Burma must be crushed!" snarled one.

"The Iravati River shall run red with blood," growled another.

"May your shadow darken the frontiers of China," thundered a third.

"But wouldn't a war so far in the East invite a revolt in Gujarat or Kabul?" asked Akbar. "And is Burma a rich enough prize to justify that risk?"

"Not in the least," said one nobleman.

"Quite a waste of our forces," said another.

"Your glory would grow by refusing to conquer so unworthy an enemy," blustered a third.

On the way home from the Council Chamber, Akbar was depressed.

"My courtiers obey me blindly, whatever I order them to do," he thought, "Since none of them dares to contradict the King, how can I know whether my plans are wise or foolish? I need to find out which of the nobles has the wisdom to correct me if my plans are bad, but the tact not to disobey my orders."

So the next morning, as the court assembled in the marble Hall of Public Audience, the King addressed his nobles, saying:

"I have decided that cats are the finest animals in the world. Do you agree?"

"By all means, *Jahanpanah*," murmured some.

"So say the sages of old," observed others.

"I have often thought of this, but lacked the wisdom to express it," chimed the rest.

"Very well," grinned Akbar. "I order each of you to keep a hundred cats. At the end of every month, you shall parade them at court—and I want to see that each man's cats are healthy, sleek, and fat!"

The noblemen bowed respectfully. But inwardly they cursed their flattering tongues.

"You had to go and agree with the King!" accused some.

"And you had to agree with those who agreed with the King!" said others.

"And you had to agree with those who agreed with those who agreed with the King!" wailed the rest.

Rich as all of them were, the noblemen calculated how much milk for a hundred cats would cost—astronomical!

Nevertheless, the Imperial edict went forth, and every courtier scrambled to furnish himself with a hundred cats. It was astonishing how the price of sleek, fat cats rose in the bazaar. A day before kittens were given away or drowned—now the mangiest stray cost more than rubies.

Every month, the courtiers paraded their precious, pampered felines before the King, who rewarded or punished them according to the seeming contentment of their cats. The nobles fretted night and day that one of their cats would lose its appetite or run away and that they would have less than a full hundred to bring to the Palace at the end of the month. And, of course, it was not long before a hundred cats became a thousand, and the courtiers were nearly driven from their homes.

"You ignore your children if they catch fever or go in ragged clothes," their wives shouted, "but if a cat skips a meal, you lose a night of sleep!"

"You just don't understand the King," they whimpered to their wives.

And the affairs of the Kingdom suffered, for the courtiers were too exhausted to fulfill their duties in the King's Council. Still the Emperor said nothing.

At length Birbal, who was allergic to cats in the first place, decided that enough was enough. Summoning his cook, he said:

"Tonight you will boil the cats' milk. Serve it to them only when it is hot enough to scald brass."

The cook did as he was ordered. When Birbal's multitude of cats approached their golden saucers, a hiss rent the air as their tongues burnt and their whiskers singed from the unexpectedly hot milk. Yowling and spitting, the cats scrambled into the shrubs and trees, and they drank not a drop of the scorching milk.

For the rest of the month Birbal kept this up, until every one of his starving cats ran from the mere sight of milk and became a sorry bag of bones.

On the day of the Emperor's cat parade, the other courtiers gawked at Birbal's sorry cats, saying:

"Now, surely, Birbal is doomed."

Akbar reviewed every cat with his usual care, rewarding and punishing the nobles, according to the happiness of their cats. But when Birbal produced his cats, the Emperor flew into a rage.

"How dare you flaunt my Royal Command? I want to see fat and healthy cats! Your animals are no more than sacks of skin! You shall be exiled for this, Birbal—or worse!"

But with respectfully downcast eyes, Birbal replied:

"O God's Shadow Upon the Earth, the problem is not with me, but with these cats. They have developed a hatred of milk. None of them will even go near it."

"Not like milk?" thundered the King. "Who ever heard of such a cat? Ridiculous."

His fingers crisped to a nearby servant. "Bring a saucer of milk at once!"

But when a plate of milk was set before Birbal's cats, the mere sight of it reminded them of scorched tongues and wilted whiskers, and they ran spitting and yowling behind curtains, beneath cushions, and even under the Peacock Throne. Then the plump cats of the other nobles waddled over to the plate of milk and licked it dry.

"Truly," said the King in wonder. "These are cats of a different color. Birbal, how do you explain it?"

Birbal smiled.

"How do you explain anything, *Jahanpanah?* Strange are the whims of cats and kings."

Unable to contain his laughter, Akbar rose, wiping the tears from his eyes, and said:

"Birbal, you have made an excellent point. You have shown, with respect and wisdom, that this was a bad idea from the start. From now on, you shall be the Chief Advisor in the King's Council. And as for the rest of you—none of you needs any longer keep a cat."

So, all the cats were driven with a vengeance from the city. And that evening there was great rejoicing—among all of Fatehpur Sikri's mice.

BIRBAL AND THE SELLER OF OIL

In the great bazaar there was an oil merchant, who was known for the fine quality and freshness of his mustard oil from Kashmir. He was always very busy.

One morning, he had sold almost all his oil and was just sitting down for a moment's rest. A flour merchant, who had been carefully eyeing all the coins the oil seller had been stuffing into his money pouch, wandered over to his stall and said:

"Give me some oil."

Rising, the oil man reached for his goatskin of oil, drained a full measure into a clay pot, sealed it, and handed it over the counter.

But, rather than take money from his own purse, the flour merchant snatched the oil man's pouch from the counter where it was resting.

"What are you doing?" cried the oil man.

"Fool! Can't you see I am taking money from my purse to pay you for the oil?"

"Your purse? That purse is mine!"

"Nonsense," sniffed the flour merchant. "This money pouch was given to me years ago by my wife. You are either a thief or mad. Keep your oil. I want nothing to do with you."

And he turned on his heel. But in a single bound the oil man leaped over his counter and seized the flour merchant by his shawl. As they scuffled, other merchants in the bazaar ran forward and dragged them apart.

"Thief!" shrieked one.

"Cheat!" howled the other.

"Quiet!" boomed a blacksmith. "We need a judge. Let us take the matter to the King."

"The King!" sneered the flour merchant. "Do you think the King has time to get mixed up in the quarrels of petty crooks like this man here?" He jabbed a derisive finger at the oil man.

"Silence!" thundered the blacksmith. "You are right. But if this is too small a matter for the King, let's go to the house of Birbal. He can solve any problem."

The flour merchant wanted to object, but all the merchants shouted "Yes! Yes!" And they marched the two enemies off in front of a cheering crowd.

Birbal invited the merchants to sit with him upon a silken rug, as courteously as if they had been nobles. He listened to the episode without interrupting. Then he glanced from one man to the other.

"Give me the purse," he commanded.

The blacksmith wrested it from the clutches of the flour merchant and offered it respectfully to Birbal.

Casually, Birbal opened the pouch, and, as he was counting the coins inside, he said: "You must be the most popular oil seller in Fatehpur Sikri?"

"I . . . I . . ." The oil man was tongue-tied in the unexpected elegance of his surroundings.

"He is," confirmed the blacksmith.

"I suppose you are extremely busy, pouring, measuring, and capping your oil?" Birbal went on.

"O Brightest Eminence," said the oil man. "From dawn to noon I have no time even to pause for a sip of rosewater."

The flour merchant smiled to himself. "This Birbal is a talkative half-wit," he thought. "He is buying time because he knows the oil man cannot prove that the money pouch is not mine."

But, even as he had these thoughts, the flour-monger felt the cold stare of Birbal upon him.

"Bring me," said Birbal to his servants, "a pot of boiling water."

Everyone exchanged puzzled glances, but when they set the pot before him, Birbal dropped the money pouch into the boiling water. Burning with curiosity, the flour merchant, the oil man, the blacksmith, and all the merchants peered into the pot as well. Before their eyes, beads of oil rose to the surface of the water, forming a sheen of rainbow-colored rings. Then Birbal pointed at the glimmering surface.

"Oil," he commented. "A money bag so drenched with oil could only belong to an oil merchant."

Staggering back, the flour merchant fell to his knees.

"Please, *Huzur*, it was only a misunderstanding . . ."

"Silence!" Birbal scolded. "You will pay the oil man seven gold *mohurs*[11] and spend forty days in jail."

There was a murmur of admiration from the assembled merchants. The flour monger hung his head, and Wazir Birbal's fame increased.

CURRYING FAVOR

Akbar loved to test Birbal's keen mind. Many jealous courtiers tried to compete with Birbal for the King's friendship, but they were in an unequal battle of wits.

One day in *durbar*, the Emperor asked Birbal:

"You were at a wedding yesterday, were you not? Tell me, Birbal, what was there to eat?"

"Let's see," mused Birbal. "There was festive rice, lentils, chicken kebabs . . ."

"What else?" asked Akbar.

"*Seer*[12] fish, yogurt and cucumbers, lamb . . ."

"What else?" asked Akbar.

"Spinach and homemade cheese, chick peas, *rotis*[13], almond sweets . . ."

At that moment, a messenger arrived from the Deccan[14] with important news for the King. The conversation with Birbal was interrupted, as Akbar went into council with his generals.

A week later in *durbar*, Akbar decided to test Birbal's memory. He turned to him without warning and said, "What else, Birbal?"

"Curry," answered Birbal promptly.

Akbar was delighted.

"Magnificent!" laughed the King. "Curry, indeed! Here, Birbal, take this emerald as a reward!"

The other courtiers, who had completely forgotten the conversation of a week ago, were baffled at what they had seen. When *durbar* was over, they met in the garden.

"Did you see the size of the emerald the Emperor gave Birbal?" asked one.

"And all Birbal said was 'curry!'" said another.

"The Emperor must truly love curry," said a third. "If he gave Birbal an emerald just for *saying* curry, what would he give for the real thing?"

"Let's give the Emperor what he wants. Then we shall all earn a fabulous reward!"

The courtiers rubbed their hands in glee.

Next day they arrived at the Hall of Public Audience carrying huge cauldrons on their heads.

"What in the world are you doing?" demanded Akbar.

"May we be your sacrifice, O Wisdom of the Age," said a courtier, laying his pot at the Emperor's feet. "We have brought you some of the delicious curry you so greatly admire." And the others fawningly set their crocks of curry before the Throne.

Akbar realized at once what was happening. He and Birbal rolled their eyes. Then the King blurted:

"You fools! Birbal was rewarded for his memory, not for curry! Now *you* shall haul the reward of your stupidity away in your stomachs. Each of you shall eat all the useless curry you have brought!"

And the Emperor and Birbal watched the miserable noblemen eat curry, and eat curry, and eat curry, until their stomachs almost burst.

GREATER THAN GOD?

Akbar grew very fond of Birbal, and, although he was a busy King, doing more in a single day than most people do in a week, he found time to chat with his new companion and learn from his ready wit. He gave Birbal money and land, so that he could live comfortably as a minister of the Crown. This aroused the envy of the many courtiers who fluttered around Akbar.

One evening, Akbar invited Birbal, and many other courtiers, to a feast. A hundred exquisite dishes were the minimum ever served for the King's repast. Yet, as Akbar looked over the ocean of food placed before him in such beautiful array, he became sad and called for his cook.

"Is it right," he asked, "for a King to have so much and only one stomach? Among my subjects there may be many empty stomachs and nothing to go in them tonight. Take some of this food into the street, and let the poor eat first. When they have been satisfied, come back and tell us, and then we will begin."

Many of the nobles were annoyed at having their dinner delayed. But Akbar called for a storyteller to keep the courtiers amused. Akbar loved stories.

The old storyteller spun many wonderful tales of long ago. Akbar rewarded him with a bag of gold. So surprised was he at the generosity of this gift, the storyteller blurted out: "Truly, *Maharaj*, you are the greatest king who ever lived. O Axis of the Earth, you are greater even than God . . ."

Immediately a mullah[15] sprang to his feet and thundered:

"That is blasphemy, *Jahanpanah!* No one can be greater than God! I demand that the storyteller be punished to the full extent of the law."

Akbar realized that the old man simply had been overexcited by the greatness of the King's reward.

"Perhaps," thought the King, "I should even have given him a little less."

Of course, God would not be affected by the old man's foolish remark. But the law against using God's name in vain was the law . . .

While Akbar was thinking these things, the storyteller grew faint with terror. The mullah shuddered in righteous indignation. Then Akbar happened to glance at Birbal, who, as usual in tense moments, wore an unfathomable half-smile.

"Your Majesty," murmured Birbal. "I do not think this is a case of blasphemy. I agree with the old man. In a way you are greater than God."

Now Akbar was really shocked. The old man had spoken foolishly. But this was Birbal! The mullah stammered angrily, unable to form words.

"How many of you," asked Akbar, turning to the rest of the assembled courtiers, "would say that your Emperor is greater than God?"

The courtiers, who had been enjoying the storyteller's discomfort, were now struck dumb. Not one of them was ready to offend God . . . but neither did any of them want to insult the King. They looked at Birbal's serene smile and then at the red-faced mullah, helpless. After a few uncomfortable moments, Akbar turned again to Birbal.

"Explain yourself!" he demanded.

"Hearing is obedience, O Brightest Eminence. We could say you are 'greater than God' in one sense, because if one of your subjects displeased you, you could exile him to a land beyond your kingdom. That, clearly, God cannot do. For the farthest emptiness of the universe is His, and He is in it, and it is in Him."

The Emperor and all his court laughed. The old storyteller sighed with relief. The sour mullah gnashed his teeth.

"In time, Birbal," said the Emperor, "you may even rid my court of flatterers, which would be a bit of good fortune never before enjoyed by any King!"

THE SWINDLING *SADHU*

In Fatehpur Sikri there lived a poor old Brahmin, whose fondest dream was to make the pilgrimage to the holy city of Varanasi before he died. So he saved what he could, working hard at whatever jobs came his way, and humbly begging when fortune was less kind.

One day, when the winter wind sawed through the frayed cloth of his ancient shawl, he thought:

"I am old, but not yet infirm. The time to make my pilgrimage has come."

He had a problem, however. The long road to Varanasi was infested with robbers—he dared not carry all his savings with him.

"If the gods permit me to return alive," he thought, "I shall need my savings to live on. But who will guard my money for me?"

He pondered and pondered, and this delayed his journey to Varanasi.

But one day, a holy mystic came to Fatehpur Sikri. This *sadhu*[16] did nothing but sit cross-legged under a banyan tree, thinking, seeing, and breathing the name of the god Rama. Many people came for his blessing, offered him coins, and joined in his prayers. He was the talk of the city.

The old Brahmin tottered by one morning with his begging bowl outstretched and saw the *sadhu* sitting like an image of stone. Suddenly, the Brahmin had an idea. Going over to the *sadhu*, he said:

"Holy brother, I am bound for the city of gods, Varanasi, but I have no family to trust my savings to. But you, who care nothing for the things of this world—my money would be safe with you."

The *sadhu* suddenly came to life, spitting fire.

"How dare you speak to me of money? Don't you know *sanyasins*[17] never touch the filthy stuff? To us it is poison. If I myself have given up such baubles of the world, why should I want to look after them for you?"

The old Brahmin fell to his knees and pleaded:

"*Maharaj*, you are a holy man. You will understand my thirst for the sight of Varanasi—it is for this alone that I have come to you."

"I cannot permit myself the touch of coin," the *sadhu* replied, "but since you speak of the yearning of your soul, I will at least watch it while you are away. Dig a hole under the banyan tree, cover your markings well, and go in peace."

"Oh, thank you, thank you," cried the old Brahmin with his eyes full of tears. "May heaven be your reward."

After many months, the Brahmin returned to Fatehpur Sikri, feeling ten years younger after his baptism in the River Ganges. He was glad to see the *sadhu* sitting exactly as he had left him. Sitting beside the holy man, the Brahmin let a respectful silence pass before raising the subject of his money. But the *sadhu* was again annoyed:

"You come straight from the holy places, and money is still on your mind! The pilgrimage has not changed you a bit. Well, go to where you buried it, and kindly take it away."

Abashed, the old Brahmin went to the banyan tree and began to dig among its roots. But he found nothing. Then he started digging in another spot. But neither was it there. The old man began to grow frantic.

"Sir, did you see anyone near that tree? My money is gone."

"I don't want to hear another word about your repulsive money!" shouted the *sadhu*. "You come here and disturb my prayers with talk of nothing but cash—next you will accuse me of stealing it—me, a holy man!"

"No," said the old beggar, "I would never say you, who have no use for worldly things, would touch my money. But I only thought—"

"Go away and never show me your face again!" shouted the *sadhu*. "And save your earthly thoughts for others."

So, shaking his head sadly, the old man wended his way.

But after a day or so, he grew so hungry from lack of money to buy even a tiny morsel, he began to think of Birbal. He was nobody, and Birbal was a great minister of state, but, still, Birbal had a reputation for helping those in trouble.

When Birbal heard the Brahmin's tale a shadow crossed his brow.

"How much money was in your purse?" he asked.

"Fifty copper *paisa*," quavered the old man.

"Not much to steal for," he said. "Still, sometimes holy men are rude, but not all rude men are holy."

And Birbal gave the old Brahmin specific instructions for the next day. Then Birbal sent him to his kitchen for food and lodged him with his servants for the night.

The next day Birbal dressed himself as a simple trader, armed himself with a chest of one hundred gold pieces, and paid a visit to the cranky *sadhu*.

"Holy brother," said Birbal, kneeling, "forgive me for disturbing your meditations, but these hundred coins of flashing gold belong to my brother, who is bound for Samarqand, and I am bound there with him. He has asked me to place them in your safe care until the day, God willing, we may return."

"Gold?" said the *sadhu*, licking his lips. "I am devoted to Rama only and never touch such filth . . ."

"I know it offends you to hear of gold," said Birbal, "But you would be doing such a kindness if you watched our treasure so we can cross the Himalayas in peace."

"Well," said the *sadhu*, his mouth a little dry. "You know I cannot touch the stuff—but if you care to bury your gold among the roots of yonder tree . . ."

But just as he was giving Birbal these instructions, the old Brahmin returned, and, remembering Birbal's orders to him, recited these words:

"Holy brother, remember me? I am back from Varanasi. Thank you for watching my bag of coppers. I have come to get them now."

"Friend!" said the *sadhu*, all smiles. "Welcome back! Blessings to you! Take your money—it is buried behind the *neem*[18] tree now, not under the banyan tree. I moved it so I could watch it all the better. Dig it up, dear brother, and long life."

The old Brahmin dug up his bag and found every coin intact. Winking at Birbal, he hobbled off in glee.

"Now," said the *sadhu*, turning back to Birbal and rubbing his palms, "the best place to bury that gold would be just there, where I can keep it in view." And he pointed a trembling finger at the *neem* tree ten paces away.

But hardly had he said these words when a servant from Birbal's house ran up to his master.

"Sir," said the servant, carefully repeating the message Birbal had taught him to say, "Your brother sends urgent word. The trip to Samarqand is off."

"Ah," smiled Birbal, picking up his chest of gold and bowing respectfully to the *sadhu*, "then I have troubled you, holy brother, in vain."

BIRBAL AND THE CROWS

B irbal's cleverness made the courtiers at Fatehpur Sikri more and more jealous of the special favor Akbar showered upon him. Almost everyone wanted to discredit him.

One day a certain court pettifogger told the Emperor that he was puzzled by a question which was truly unanswerable, probably even by Birbal. Curious, Akbar asked Birbal to try. The courtier, prepared for an easy victory, let his question fly.

"How many crows are there in Fatehpur Sikri, exactly?"

Birbal answered promptly.

"Three million, two hundred twenty thousand, seven hundred and ninety-four."

"Just a moment," said Akbar, leaning forward from the Peacock Throne. "What proof have you that there are exactly that many crows in the city?"

"If you don't believe it, O Full Moon, have this courtier of yours go out and count them. He will find exactly the number of crows I have stated."

"Yes," persisted the Great Mughal, "but suppose he finds fewer?"

"Obviously that will mean that some of the city crows have left town to visit their relatives."

"And if he discovers more?"

"In that case, their relatives from the county will have come to town to visit them."

THE THIEF'S STICK

A rich merchant of Fatehpur Sikri presented himself at Birbal's house, complaining of the theft of ten *mohurs*.

"Whom do you suspect?" asked Birbal.

"To tell the truth, sir," said the merchant. "It must be one of my servants, for the money was kept in a secret place in my kitchen, and nobody could have broken in without their noticing. I have threatened them with lashes and imprisonment, but—"

"Threats do not lead to the truth," interrupted Birbal. "How many servants do you employ?"

"Seven, *Huzur*," replied the merchant.

"Make sure they are all at home tomorrow morning."

And the next day Birbal called at the merchant's splendid mansion, accompanied by a half-naked holy man, with matted hair and wild eyes. Merchant and servants alike were terrified at the sight of him.

"There has been a theft in this home," Birbal began gravely, "and so I have enlisted the services of this famous wizard."

With these words the magician took seven sticks of equal length from a camelhair bag, muttered a spell, and blew upon them with a crazed stare.

Handing one stick to each of the servants, Birbal said:

"By the power of this wizard, the mere touch of a thief will cause any one of these sticks to grow an inch's length overnight. Now each of you shall be locked in a separate chamber, and tomorrow we shall examine your sticks."

The servants shuddered, as each was conducted to his quarters.

When Birbal returned the following day and gathered the servants together, he told the merchant:

"Measure the stick of every man."

When he did so, he turned to Birbal in astonishment.

"*Huzur*, this is amazing—none of the sticks has grown, but the cook's is one inch shorter!"

"Then," smiled Birbal, "the cook is the thief. Only a man tormented by a guilty conscience would believe the fairy tale of magical sticks—and so he cut his stick shorter during the night."

And so the merchant recovered his money, and the fame of Birbal grew.

NEITHER HERE NOR THERE

In the beautiful city of Fatehpur Sikri, Akbar built a palace called The House of Worship. There, every Friday night, scholars, poets, and philosophers gathered from every nation in the world—even from faraway Europe. To the delight of the Emperor they discussed problems of logic and metaphysics far into the night.

One evening a dervish[19] presented himself to this august assembly and said:

"I have traveled from kingdom to kingdom, and everywhere I have defeated the wisest men in debate. Every king has given me an amulet of gold as a present, and so far I have collected forty-nine of them. When I defeat the wise men of Fatehpur Sikri, I shall win the fiftieth."

"Let us see," smiled Akbar. "Pose us a problem."

"My challenge is this:

"*Bring here before us a thing which is here but not there;*
"*Another which is there but not here;*
"*A third which is neither here nor there;*
"*And a fourth which is in both places.*"

The wise men of Akbar's court were stunned. But Birbal stepped forward and said:

"I will return in one hour."

The moon had risen above the lovely parapets of Fatehpur Sikri when Birbal returned with three men: a thief, a *sadhu* (or holy man), and a beggar.

"Sire," Birbal began. "The dervish has asked for a thing which is here but not there. This first man is a thief. He lives on the earth among us. But he steals and cheats. He does not repent. So his prayers do not reach heaven, and neither will his soul. He is here, but not there."

And, saddened by his doom, the thief slunk away into the night.

"Next," said Birbal, "something which is there but not here. This *sadhu* does not think about this world of cares at all. He only sits and thinks about God. He is so heavenly minded, he is no earthly good. He is there but not here."

The *sadhu* stood impassive, as if he had heard not a word which had been spoken.

"Go on," said Akbar, smiling.

"This beggar is neither here nor there," said Birbal. "He does not enjoy this life, because he is poor. So he always dreams of another, better life. But he is content to beg, so he never improves his lot—he just envies those who succeed. He is neither here nor there."

The Emperor nodded sadly.

"But what about something which is both here and there?" he asked.

"This man," said Birbal. "Is none other than yourself, *Maharaj*. Even if you were not a king, you would be a generous man. He who gives all he has to others enjoys this world because those in it respect and love him. But, because he is not attached to wealth, or even to what other people think of him, his contentment will abide in the next world as well. He is both here and there."

Smiling, the dervish let all of the forty-nine amulets slip from his arms and fall ringing to the marble floor.

"Let Your Majesty rejoice," he said, "for his court is adorned with the rarest pearl of wisdom in the world."

HEAVEN'S GIFTS

"It is strange," said Jai Mal in the Hall of Public Audience, "that Heaven should be so careless in the distribution of its blessings. One would think that God, in giving Birbal the gift of matchless wit, would have chosen somebody of noble birth or handsome features to receive it. Birbal is clever indeed, but I fear he somewhat resembles a donkey!"

There was laughter among the whole assembly, and Jai Mal preened himself at having humiliated Akbar's favorite.

The King was annoyed at such blunt rudeness, but Birbal replied:

"There is a reason for that, O Ocean of Bright Promise. Before we were born, the angels took us to the Treasure House of God and asked us to choose from among the many gifts of heaven.

"In one pavilion were stored the benefits of Wealth, and many souls gathered there, collecting as much as they could.

"In another pavilion were Beauty and Personal Charm, and other souls loaded themselves with these.

"But in a smaller pavilion, covered with cobwebs and overlooked, the riches of Intelligence were kept. I was so fascinated with these that by the time I had finished scooping them up, the other pavilions had been emptied, and our generation was delivered upon the earth.

"Now, I may have come to resemble a donkey, perhaps from living among you rich and handsome courtiers who always play the donkey's part, but at least my words ring sweetly in the Emperor's ears, even as your braying causes him to stop them up!"

And Akbar laughed, as Jai Mal gnashed his teeth.

THE EGG HUNT

Akbar's courtiers were truly miserable at Birbal's success. So the Emperor decided to lift their spirits by playing his own trick on Birbal.

One day at court, he sent Birbal away on an errand. Then he had a servant bring a basket of eggs. He told the assembled grandees:

"Each of you take one egg. Later, when I tell you to dive into the garden pool, you will pretend that you each found an egg at the bottom. Understand?"

"Yes, *Jahanpanah*," said the courtiers sadly.

"The Emperor has gone mad," they thought.

But when Birbal returned from his errand, Akbar said:

"Last night I had a dream. I dreamed I should test you all to find out which of you is truly noble and which not fit to live at my court. The dream told me I should command each of you to dive into the garden pool. The worthy men would all find an egg at the bottom. But those who came up without an egg should be banished."

And the Emperor led everyone into the garden for the test. The courtiers were delighted.

"Now it is Birbal's time to lose," they grinned.

But Birbal noticed their whispering and thought, "Something is up."

One by one, the courtiers dived into the reflecting pond. One by one, they came up from among the water lilies holding an egg.

"Here, Your Majesty," they said, happily offering the eggs to the King. When Birbal's turn came at last, he thought, "There must be a basket of eggs at the bottom." So he unwrapped his turban and dove into the pond.

He groped through the dark water but found no basket of eggs. When his breath gave out, he burst to the surface, empty-handed.

"What?" cried Akbar angrily. "No egg?"

But instead of answering, Birbal climbed up on the garden wall and started to crow.

"He's lost his mind," said the courtiers. "It's the first time he's been defeated, and it's driven him mad."

Birbal crowed again.

"What are you doing, Birbal?" asked the Emperor.

"Why surely it's obvious," said Birbal gesturing to the gaggle of soaking courtiers, "that among so many wet hens you will find at least one rooster!"

BIRBAL AND THE
KING OF AFGHANISTAN

J ai Mal and the other nobles continued to hatch plots against the
Nine Sages of Akbar's court.

Besides Birbal, one of these Nine Sages was Tansen. He was the
minstrel of magical prowess. The jealous courtiers thought that if they
could eliminate both of these upstarts at one stroke, so much the better.

They told the Emperor that cleverness and talent could not overpower
the irrevocable force of destiny.

"Give me an example," said Akbar.

They told him the case of a young prince, who had been sent by one
king to another, bearing a secret message which asked that the second
king, as a favor to the first, put the young prince to death.

"Nobody could escape such a trap," they said. "Not Tansen. Nor even
Birbal."

Nothing is more dangerous than the curiosity of kings. Akbar decided
to challenge Tansen and Birbal. He wrote to Mirza Mohammed Hakim,
his half-brother, the King of Afghanistan.

"Dear Brother," wrote Akbar, "the men bringing you this message are
the worst criminals in my realm. Show your loyalty to me by having them
killed."

Then he called Birbal and Tansen, gave them the sealed letter, and
sped them on their fatal mission.

When the Afghan King read the letter, he crisped his fingers, and the
messengers were thrown into the darkest dungeon. Tansen was sick with
fear.

"What a miserable fate has overtaken us!" he cried. "Here we lie,
condemned to die for no reason whatever."

Birbal, however, merely shrugged. When the day of execution dawned, he took Tansen by the sleeve and said:

"When the moment comes for us to die, you watch me and do everything I do."

"Oh, yes, *baba*[20]," cried Tansen, "if you think we can be saved."

They were led to the block. A huge executioner stood by, handling his shiny ax as if it itched in his palms. The King was about to give the order to chop, when Birbal ran forward and placed his head at the royal feet.

"Please, Majesty, whatever you do, kill me first!"

The King said: "If you want that, so be it. Anyway, both of you have only minutes to live."

But hardly had he finished speaking when Tansen also rushed forward, prostrated himself, and wailed:

"O God's Shadow on Earth, please grant my last wish and kill *me* before you kill *him!*"

And both of them pleaded and made such a noise that the King had to shout for silence.

"Both of you are on the brink of Eternal Night," he thundered. "What possible difference does it make which of you the ax cleaves last?"

Neither prisoner spoke. Great beads of sweat ran down Tansen's neck.

"Listen," said the King, "whichever of you explains why you want to die first, I will kill him before the other."

Tansen looked at Birbal in bewilderment. Birbal at last spoke up.

"You see, Highness," he murmured, "it is a matter of astrology."

"Astrology?" sneered the King.

"Yes, Sire," said Birbal. "According to the stars, whoever is executed in Kabul—just at this precise moment—will come back in his next life as Conqueror of Afghanistan."

"What!" The King rose from his throne.

"Yes, Sire," said Birbal. "Now please, since I have told you the secret, give your Crown to me in my next life. Let me die first."

When the King heard these words, he glared first at one ragged prisoner, then at the other. Rubbing his huge beard, he thought, "This is Akbar's trick to take over my Kingdom without a war."

And clapping his hands, he ordered:

"Execution indefinitely postponed."

BIRBAL'S JOURNEY TO PARADISE

The court barber nursed his hatred for Birbal and plotted daily against him. Finally, he hit on a plan. When the Emperor Akbar next called him to trim his beard, he said:

"You know, *Jahanpanah*, last night I dreamed about your father."

The Great Mughal at once took interest.

"Tell me what he said to you."

"He is very happy in Paradise, but he says that all the inhabitants of Heaven are terrible bores. He would like you to send him someone who can talk to him and keep him amused."

Of course no one possessed a wit like Birbal's, and, although Akbar prized him very much, to appease his poor father in Paradise, he would consent to give Birbal up. Naturally, the only way of reaching Heaven is through death.

When Birbal responded to the Emperor's summons, Akbar said:

"I think you love me, Birbal, enough to make any sacrifice for my sake."

"You know I do, *Jahanpanah*."

"Then I would like you to go to Heaven and keep my dear father company."

"Very well," Birbal said evenly, "but please give me a few days to prepare."

"Certainly," said the King, delighted. "You are doing me a great favor. I will give you a week."

Birbal went home and dug a deep pit, which would serve as his own grave. But he also excavated a secret tunnel that opened under the floor of his house. Then he returned to the Imperial Court.

"*Maharaj*," he said, "in accordance with an old family tradition, I would like to be buried near my house—and, if you don't mind, I would like to be buried alive. I have heard that is a less painful way to die."

So, to the great happiness of the court barber, Birbal was buried alive. Of course, Birbal made his way at once through the tunnel into his own house, where he stayed in hiding for six months, neither going out in the sun nor touching a razor.

At the end of that time, with his hair and beard grown long and shaggy, he came out of hiding and obtained an audience with the Great Mughal.

"Birbal!" cried the Emperor.

"It's Birbal's ghost!" shrieked the courtiers, trembling at his pale skin and wild mane.

"No, no," smiled Birbal, extending his arms. "Feel my hands. Touch my beard. It is I."

"Where have you come from?" asked Akbar, peering at him keenly.

"From Paradise, Majesty. I spent such a lovely time with your father that he asked God to give me special permission to return to earth."

Akbar was astounded.

"But this is a miracle," he said. "Did the old Emperor give you any message for me?"

"Just one, O Peacock of the Age. Do you see my whiskers and long hair?"

Akbar nodded.

"Well, it seems very few barbers make it to Heaven. Your father asks you to send him yours at once."

VOLUME 2

A Caravan From Hindustan:
More Birbal Tales from the Oral Traditions of India

THE SEARCH FOR BIRBAL

One summer all India was parched and gasping because the monsoons[21] did not come. Akbar consulted the wise men of the land, who took counsel together and finally proclaimed:

"The drought will not end until Wazir Birbal laughs."

So the Emperor summoned Birbal and said:

"I command you to laugh."

But Birbal was not a person to laugh for nothing.

"Neither laughter nor the heart's desire is at the command of kings," said Birbal. "Everything has a reason of its own."

Akbar was deeply offended at this disobedience, and as punishment he banished Birbal from the capital.

So Birbal wandered the countryside in the fearful heat, helping the country folk he met with his wise suggestions, and living on the bread and *paneer*[22] they offered him.

One day he was lying in a field in the shadow of a haystack when he heard the quavering voices of two old people nearby. It was an ancient farmer and his wife. They had just come to rest on the other side of the haystack after a hard morning's work in their fields. The old woman sighed:

"The earth itself is crying for relief. When will the monsoon come?"

"When Wazir Birbal laughs," said the old man.

"But *how* will he laugh?" asked his wife. "He has been banished by the King. He is far from the devoted attentions of his wife. What could possibly make him laugh now?"

"If his wife is anything like *you*," sputtered the old man, "banishment will make him *die* laughing!"

"Well!" shouted the old woman. "At least Birbal's wife doesn't have a fool for a husband!"

And the old woman started pelting the old man with clods of dirt.

But both of them froze at the sound of full-throated laughter from the other side of the haystack—and no sooner had they heard it, than a fat droplet sizzled in the dust. *Splash!* came another and then another and another, until the heavens pealed and the clouds burst, and the leaves pattered joyfully for the overdue blessing of the monsoon.

From a balcony in the mighty Red Fort at Agra, the Emperor heard the crash of thunder and the grateful music of the garden birds and watched the ruffling of raindrops upon the River Jumna like a thousand falling coins. Akbar knew that Wazir Birbal had laughed.

But even as the fields turned green again and smiles returned to peasant homes, day after day passed with no word or sign of Birbal. And the King grew lonely. There were thousands of villages throughout his Empire where Birbal might be staying, but how could Akbar know to which he should send the royal summons for his friend? After pondering many days, he made a plan.

Akbar issued an edict that all the village headmen from a hundred miles around should report to Agra to pay their respects—but the Emperor commanded that none should present himself unless he was "half in sunlight and half in shade."

The village headmen were baffled, but they did their best to comply with the Imperial order.

The Emperor watched from the ramparts, suppressing his laughter, as he saw them approach the city gates, hopping from tree to tree or holding their turbans unraveled above their heads.

But then he spied a village chief striding confidently in the morning sun—for over his head he held a string cot. As the sun shone through the cot's weave, a checkered shadow fell upon his shoulders—he was actually walking half in sunlight and half in shade.

"Bring that man to me," said Akbar. "Only Birbal could have given him such clever advice. But we will make sure."

When the village headman had paid homage, the Emperor entrusted him with a goat.

"Keep this animal with you for a month and feed him every day at my expense. At the end of a month, you must return him to me. If he has *gained* an ounce or *lost* an ounce, you shall lose your head."

The village headman wailed to his companions as he led the Emperor's goat home:

"What terrible luck, taking that stranger's advice about the cot! Now instead of a reward, I must die—for who can feed a goat every day without his gaining weight?"

But when Birbal heard the headman's problem, he laughed. So the King was out to find him!

Birbal said:

"Capture a tiger and place him in a cage. Then tie the goat next to the tiger and feed him every day."

"Capture a tiger!" exploded the headman. "That's easy for you to say, but see where your advice has landed me already!"

"Well, it's your head," said Birbal calmly. "And I'm sure that there are a few other people in this village who would like to become headman when you are gone . . ."

Whiskers bristling, the headman looked suspiciously at the sun-burnt faces all around him.

"All right," he growled, "we'll capture a tiger."

After many adventures, and with Birbal's help, they clapped a snarling tiger in a cage and tied the goat right beside it. The goat ate everything they fed it for a whole month. But night and day the yellow eyes of the tiger burned hungrily, and the big cat greedily licked its lips. And night and day the little goat's knees knocked in terror.

On the appointed day, the village headman returned the goat to the Imperial Court. Todar Mal, the King's treasurer, weighed the animal and announced:

"It has neither lost an ounce nor gained an ounce."

The headman heaved a sigh of relief, gratefully massaging his neck, and Akbar smiled. Now he was sure that Birbal was hiding in this headman's village. So he said:

"Return to your home, headman, but hear my command. Next month my armies will overrun the shores of Orissa. My Empire will then reach from the Arabian Sea to the Bay of Bengal, and there will be a great celebration for the marriage of the two seas in my kingdom. In honor of this event, you shall arrange for all the rivers in your territory to approach my palace."

The headman's knees sank beneath him, and, leading the goat back home, he was so sick with fear he could hardly speak.

"See what misfortune the Emperor singles out for me!" he sobbed to Birbal. "I think destiny is conspiring to deprive me of my head."

But Birbal laughed, thought a moment, and sent the headman back on the long and weary road to Agra.

Presenting himself again before the Throne, the headmen waveringly said to Akbar:

"Most Auspicious Majesty, the rivers of my territory have agreed to come, but they ask that you command all the wells in your kingdom to come halfway out to meet them."

Chuckling, the Emperor responded:

"I will certainly do so, but I must place upon you a further demand. Since I perceive such rare abilities in the people of your village, I would like you to return in fifteen days, bringing me as a gift a potful of wisdom."

"Oh brutal fate! O cruel world!" cried the village headmen as he trudged along the homeward road. "How lucky are those headmen who never earn the attention of a king! What am I to do? What can he possibly mean by a potful of wisdom, and where am I to get it?"

When Birbal heard of the headman's new calamity, he went off walking through the fields with his head bowed in thought. Some time later, he returned to the headman's hut, only to find the villagers preparing for the headman's funeral. Birbal laughed:

"I've got you out of three scrapes—don't you trust me for the fourth?"

"It isn't *your* neck," groaned the village headman. "But let's hear what you have to say."

"Bring a small, clay pot," he said, "and follow me."

The headman stared at Birbal, his mouth agape.

"Do as I say," laughed Birbal.

So the headman took a clay pot, and the whole village trooped after Birbal into the fields.

Birbal came to a pumpkin vine, whose flowers had faded and whose little pumpkins had just begun to grow. He took the clay pot and placed one of the tiny, baby pumpkins inside. Then he stood up and triumphantly brushed off his hands.

The village headman looked at Birbal expectantly.

"Now wait," said Birbal.

"Wait?" asked the headman.

"Yes, wait." said Birbal.

Crestfallen, the village headman trudged back to his hut. And his family went on planning his funeral.

But by the fourteenth day, the pumpkin had grown to its full measure and could not be taken out of the pot. Birbal cut it away from the creeping vine and said to the headman:

"Take this to Akbar."

Covering the mouth of the pot with cheese cloth, the doubtful headman tramped back to Agra and prostrated himself before the King. Then he spoke the words Birbal had given him to say:

"Here is a miraculous pot, O Refuge of the World, containing the wisdom you desired. Please take its wisdom out for yourself, for in our village we know how to fill it with wisdom again. But do not break the pot or crush the wisdom it contains, because then all the wisdom of *your* Kingdom will be lost."

Trembling with mirth, the King shouted to his stable master:

"Bring my favorite elephant!"

And placing the village headman on a camel, the King set out in regal splendor from the shimmering city. The fields were emerald green from the gentle rains, and the singing of frogs in the rice terraces spoke for all of nature's joy.

When the procession had reached the tiny village, the King descended. Surrounded by his generals, he suddenly turned on the headman and thundered:

"Criminal! You will now bring my minister Birbal to me! Through these many ruses, I discovered that you have kidnapped him! You are holding him in this village! Now let him go!"

"Kidnapped!" squalled the headman, sinking to his knees. "Oh, but Sire . . ."

At these words, Birbal emerged from one of the huts.

"The headman is innocent, *Jahanpanah*," said Birbal.

"I know," smiled Akbar. "It was the last test—so you would come out."

The village headman collapsed into the arms of his wife. And Akbar embraced his friend with great rejoicing.

A feast was prepared such as no village had ever known, and after many days of making merry, the Emperor and Birbal returned to Agra, leaving a thousand golden *mohurs* for the village headman and his people.

And Akbar never banished Birbal again.

A SOUND INVESTMENT

One day a very poor man was sitting outside a popular kebab shop. As the aroma of grilling meat wafted into the street, the beggar blissfully inhaled, sighing with ecstasy again and again. The owner of the shop noticed the beggar's sniffing his kebabs and was annoyed.

"You there!" he shouted. "If you are going to sit there and enjoy smelling my food, pay me!"

"I'm not harming anyone," answered the poor man as bravely as he could. But the owner of the kebab shop was a burly, short-tempered fellow, and he scooped the offender up by the scruff of his neck.

"We'll see about that," he bellowed. "I'm taking you to the judge! He won't tolerate lazy riffraff hanging about the shops of respectable merchants!"

The poor man, frail with hunger, could do no more than plead and protest, and a great crowd gathered as he was dragged mercilessly to the house of the famed judge—Birbal.

Birbal listened to the facts of the case in silence. When everyone had finished arguing, he turned to the poor man and frowned.

"How much money do you have?" asked Birbal.

Trembling, the beggar held up the smallest possible copper coin and whimpered, "Good sir, please, this is all I have in the world."

"Give it here," demanded Birbal.

"*Huzur*, have mercy on a helpless—"

"Give it here!" boomed Birbal. The crowd hushed. Miserably, the old man surrendered his only coin to the judge, who then turned to the fat, triumphant merchant.

"I want you to listen very carefully now," said Birbal.

The room was noiseless. The kebab seller beetled his brows.

With a *ping!* Birbal bounced the tiny copper coin off the judge's bench.

"Did you hear that?" he asked, smiling.

"Yes . . ." answered the kebab seller.

"Well, you are repaid for the *scent* of your grilled meat by the *sound* of this poor man's coin."

And returning the copper coin the beggar, he announced:

"Case dismissed!"

BIRBAL THE HISTORIAN

One day Akbar called Birbal to him. He was an illiterate ruler, but he loved hearing the stories of old.

"I have been having the *Mahabharata*[23] read to me just now," said the Great Mughal, "and I was thinking. The five Pandava brothers had this wonderful epic written about their lives . . . why shouldn't there also be an epic poem about me?"

"A noble thought, Your Majesty," murmured Birbal.

"Yes," said the King. "You can call it the *Akbar-nama*[24]. Start writing it at once."

"Yes, *Jahanpanah*," said Birbal. He wondered what "meaningful" challenge Akbar would set for him next, but aloud he said:

"Please give me one month."

"Granted," smiled the King.

At the appointed time, Birbal appeared at court, without having written a single word of his assignment. Under his arm he carried a thick ream of blank pages.

"O Peacock of the Age, the book is finished except for some minor details. In order to complete it, please grant me a brief interview with the Queen, so that I can know some important facts about your personal life."

"Fine," said Akbar, "if it is necessary for my epic."

Now the famous Pandava brothers of the *Mahabharata* all shared a common wife, the beautiful Draupadi. So Birbal said to the Queen:

"*Begum Sahiba*, I am collecting information about the Emperor in order to write a book like the story of the Pandavas. So I need to know if you have had as many lovers as Draupadi . . ."

The Queen, outraged at such a suggestion, seized the blank manuscript and flung it into the fire.

"Tell the King to ask me himself if he wants to know how much I love him!" she cried. "I am a faithful wife, and I will not tolerate such jealous tricks and spies!"

Birbal watched the pages curl in the flames and drift up the chimney in spiraling smoke. He shrugged and returned to the Emperor.

When Akbar saw the Imperial Historian, he jumped up from the Peacock Throne, rubbing his hands.

"Well, let me see it! Where is my *Akbar-nama?*"

"The Queen has thrown it into the fire," said Birbal complacently.

"What!" sputtered the Mughal. "But why?"

"I really haven't any idea, *Huzur*. I asked her a simple question and she became hysterical."

"But what shall I do for my *Akbar-nama?*" wailed the King.

"*Jahanpanah*," smiled Birbal, "lesser rulers may write history. You, O Full Moon, should be content to make it."

And, smiling thoughtfully, the Emperor agreed.

THE IMPERIAL MANGOES

Akbar had a special mango tree that produced the finest fruit in all India. However, people were always stealing it. So he constructed seven circular fences around the tree, each fence inside another. In every fence was a gate, and at each gate he placed a guard.

But he still wondered if his mangoes were safe. So he asked Birbal: "Do you think *you* could steal fruit from that tree?"

Birbal thought a moment, smiled, and said, "Most assuredly."

"Then try," said the King.

"I will show you, Sire, if you will help me carry out the theft . . . in disguise, of course."

"Agreed," smiled the King.

That night, Birbal and the King approached the guards disguised as wandering dervishes.

"I will offer each guard a bribe," whispered Birbal.

"Will *my* guards take bribes?" asked the King, astonished.

"Sire," smiled Birbal, "they would hardly be guards if they would *not.*"

The King grunted.

Approaching the first guard, Birbal said, "If you will let me take some fruit from that tree, I will give you half of what I steal, if you promise to give me only one mango in return."

To the Emperor's chagrin, the guard readily agreed, and the two approached the next gate.

To the second guard, Birbal said, "If you will let me take some fruit from that tree, I will give you half of what I steal, if you promise to give me only one mango in return."

The second guard agreed.

To the third guard, Birbal said, "If you will let me take some fruit from that tree, I will give you half of what I steal, if you promise to give me only one mango in return."

The third guard agreed.

And Birbal made the same deal with the fourth guard, the fifth, the sixth and the seventh.

Finally, he and the King stood beneath the magnificent mango tree. Akbar was perplexed.

"How many mangoes do we need?" he asked.

"Just two," grinned Birbal.

"What!" exclaimed Akbar. "After all the mangoes we've promised in bribes?"

"Watch, Sire," smiled Birbal.

And taking a pair of the ripest, he walked up to the seventh guard, gave him one mango, and asked for one back. The guard started to bluster, but Birbal reminded him of his deal, and the disguised King gleefully testified that it was so.

Then, with the same two mangoes, he walked up to the sixth guard, gave him one mango, and asked for one back.

Then he walked up to the fifth guard, gave him one mango, and asked for one back.

And he did the same with the fourth guard, the third, the second and the first.

When the two "thieves" had passed by each of the fuming guards and had exited the outermost gate, Birbal handed one of the two mangoes to his royal companion and said:

"The fruit, *Jahanpanah*, of our labors."

Akbar threw his head back in laughter.

"I ought to have them all flogged," he choked, wiping tears of mirth from his eyes, "but it's too funny seeing them all standing there empty-handed!"

And the two friends strolled through the starlit night, listening to the call of nightingales, and sucking the delicate nectar of the Imperial fruit.[25]

FEAST FOR THE LAZY

The Emperor Akbar often gave feasts to certain of his subjects. At times he would announce a banquet for the disabled. Sometimes he commanded a feast for widows or for old soldiers or for orphans. One day he said to Birbal:

"It occurs to me that there is one group of people whom I have never benefited—let us feast all the lazy-bones in our kingdom!"

Birbal laughed.

"As you wish, *Maharaj*."

The edict went forth, and soon an immense army of people collected under a brightly-colored tent which had been erected in front of the palace. Watching this huge assembly from a balcony, Akbar said:

"Birbal, I find it hard to believe that everyone here is truly lazy. Some of them must be faking. They are taking advantage of the laziness of others. How can this be tested?"

Birbal laughed, thought for a moment, and then sent word to the royal chefs:

"Delay serving the food."

Before long, the guests had begun to grumble.

"If he is not going to give us anything to eat, why has the Emperor make this announcement? For show only?"

At that moment, Birbal set the tent on fire.

Forgetting their stomach pangs, the malcontents fled for their lives. Only a tiny handful of guests paid no attention to the stampede, remaining utterly indifferent and at their ease.

When servants had put the fire out, Birbal grinned and said:

"These, *Huzur*, are the people you wished to benefit—men too lazy to run for their lives! The others were mere impostors."

Laughing heartily, the Emperor fed them well.

THE EMPEROR'S DREAM

S ome courtiers were complaining bitterly to Akbar.

"Your Highness indulges Birbal in everything. Even bad news you welcome, so long as it comes from his lips."

"Ah," said the King. "That is because he always finds a *useful* way to give me even bad news."

"Mere flattery," replied the courtiers.

"It is more than that," said Akbar. "When an occasion arises, I shall demonstrate what I mean."

A week later, Akbar addressed the assembled *diwan*:

"I had a dream last night that all my teeth but one had fallen out. What is the interpretation of this vision?"

The fortune-tellers put their heads together and finally said:

"This dream means that all Your Majesty's relatives will die before you."

Akbar frowned.

"Bad news for a dynasty," he said. Then turning to Birbal he asked, "How would you read the dream?"

"I would say," said Birbal slowly, "that you, of all your family, will enjoy the longest life."

"Now," asked the Emperor, turning to the jealous courtiers, "how would *you* rather hear it said?"

THE KING'S SEAL

Akbar liked to know what his subjects were saying among themselves—about himself and about their own lives. So he used to disguise himself as a common person and wander the streets of Fatehpur Sikri by night. He had many wonderful adventures this way and learned first-hand of the most pressing dreams and problems of his people.

But Birbal often cautioned against these wanderings.

"The life of an Emperor is the heart of the Empire. It is too dangerous for you to wander the city streets alone."

"If the city by night is too dangerous for a man alone, the fault is the King's. I should know the cause of this danger and correct it."

One evening, when Akbar felt like adventure, he donned the guise of an ancient dervish. Slipping through the back gate of the palace, he threaded through the fog-veiled streets.

After a few short moments, he felt the shiver of unseen eyes upon him. Somebody was following him in the empty bazaar.

Glancing over his shoulder, he saw the vague shadow of a shabby-looking man. When Akbar stopped, the man stopped and pretended to look into a wine shop. Touching the hilt of his dagger with his hand, the King went boldly forward to question him. He turned out to be a one-eyed fellow with a ragged beard—just the sort of footpad whom the guards should never have let through the city gates.

"What is your name?" demanded Akbar.

"Wanderlust," came the reply.

"Where do you live?"

"Everywhere."

"How do you earn your keep?"

"By roaming from one end of the earth to the other and gathering its wisdom."

"Hmm," thought Akbar, not liking these evasive replies. "This man is challenging me. Let me put him to the test."

"Since you claim to be wise," he said aloud, "let me ask you a riddle."

"Ask," said the one-eyed man.

The King quoted a poem.

> *Where I will, I wander, yet I have no home.*
> *I have crossed the seas and scaled heaven's dome.*
> *Though never beheld, I am felt by all*
> *And mine is the voice of the clarion's call.*
> *The world would lie as still as death*
> *Without the fragrance of my breath.*
> *Who am I?*

Without hesitation, the stranger replied:

"The wind."

And hardly had these words left his lips than he posed a riddle to the King:

> *Like the wandering wind am I,*
> *But I have roamed* beyond *the sky,*
> *Yes, to the very Throne of God,*
> *And, yet, I live, like a pea in a pod,*
> *In a cave whose only source of light*
> *Is two small holes, shining bright.*
> *Who, then, am I?*

And without hesitation, Akbar answered:

"The mind."

And so began a duel of wits between the King in disguise and the one-eyed stranger.

"What is the keenest weapon?" asked the stranger.

"The intellect," replied Akbar. "And who is the greatest fool?"

"He who does not know where his own welfare lies," said the stranger. "And how do you recognize a fool?"

"By his speech," said Akbar. "And who is the unconquerable foe?"

"Death," said the stranger. "But what lives forever?"

"Fame," replied Akbar. "And which two neighbors never see each other?"

"The eyes," replied the stranger. "But what sleeps with its eyes open?"

"A fish," said Akbar. "And what is reborn after its birth?"

"The moon," answered the stranger. "And what is not thought of until it is lost?"

"Health," said Akbar. "And what is the friend of the dying man?"

"The charity he did in his lifetime," said the stranger. "And what makes one wealthy if it is cast away?"

"Greed," said Akbar. "But what is the hardest enemy to overcome?"

"Anger," said the stranger. "And what is it men call good fortune?"

"The result of what they have honestly done," said Akbar. "But who is truly happy?"

"The man without debts," said the stranger. "And what is hypocrisy?"

"Setting religious standards for others," said Akbar. "And what is the greatest wonder of them all?"

"Every day Death gathers lives beyond counting, yet those who live think: Death cannot come this day for me. But what," said the stranger, "is the rarest thing?"

"To know when to stop," said Akbar. "And what is there in this world which neither Sun nor Moon can see?"

"Darkness," said the stranger, "And why is it said the difference between truth and falsehood is that between the ears and eyes?"

"Whatever you see with the eyes is truth, and whatever you hear with the ears is falsehood," said Akbar. "And how can you make a line shorter without erasing either end?"

"Draw a longer line beside it," said the stranger, "and the first will then be shorter. And how can you separate a mixture of sugar and sand?"

Now Akbar was stumped. He thought and he thought, but he could not come up with an answer to this problem. So at last the stranger told him:

"Wash it in water, which will carry away the sugar, leaving the sand behind."

"Come with me," the Emperor smiled. "I shall dress you in fine robes and give you a splendid reward."

"A likely story," sneered the one-eyed man. "You are probably no more than a common thief, trying to lure me into your clutches. Be gone, before I beat you black and blue!"

"Is this how you repay a kindness?" thundered Akbar. "Know that your insolence is spoken to none other than Jalaludin Mohammed Akbar Padshah Ghazi, Emperor of Hindustan!"

"You, the Emperor?" laughed the one-eyed man. "Now I've heard everything!"

"But I am!" shouted Akbar, turning red-faced. And pulling the Ring of the Royal Seal from his finger, he handed it to the stranger and said: "Inspect that ring and weep. For your impudence will cost your head!"

Well, the stranger recognized the Seal all right. But no sooner had he taken it in his fist than he bolted down the street. Shocked, Akbar bounded after him, crying:

"Thief! Thief! Don't let him escape!"

Some merchants standing around a kabob shop heard the call and tackled the one-eyed man as he passed. But when the Emperor came panting up, he heard the stranger say:

"Back off, presumptuous ones! Observe my Ring and kneel, for I am none other than Jalaludin Mohammed Akbar Padshah Ghazi, Emperor of Hindustan!"

Recognizing the ring, and aware of Akbar's love of wandering the city in disguise, the merchants fell to the ground to beg their Emperor's pardon.

Alarmed, Akbar realized that the one-eyed man would probably order the merchants to seize him. Swiftly he melted into the shadows.

Sadly trudging back to the palace, Akbar entered his apartments through a secret passage, worried sick about the loss of the Royal Seal—armies could be raised, treasures paid, and kingdoms given away at the mere sight of it. But just as he was wrestling with these worries, he noticed a small parcel on his bed.

Opening it in haste, a wave of relief passed over him when he found inside—the Ring of the Royal Seal!

With the ring was a note, which he unfolded at once and read:

"I may have acted the part of a thief, but perhaps I have shown your Majesty how vulnerable even an Emperor is, alone in the shadowy world beyond the palace. A King may lose worse things than his Seal—even his head.

—Your obedient servant, Birbal."

"I should have known!" thought Akbar smiling, "That clever, one-eyed dog could only have been one man!"

And although Akbar never gave up his habit of wandering disguised among his subjects, from that day on, a disguised Wazir Birbal always traveled at his side.

THE WICKED JUDGE

The judge in Delhi was a dishonest man, although his flowing white beard and venerable turban made him appear pious.

One day a poor old widow came to him with a request.

"I have decided to make the long pilgrimage to Mecca, sir. Please keep this bag in your custody while I am gone."

Looking up from the holy scriptures, the judge seemed unconcerned. "What is in the bag?" he asked.

"Sir, my life savings. I may die upon the journey, but I am afraid to take them with me, and I have no safe place to leave them behind."

"Madam," said the judge frowning. "I am an Imperial Officer—it is an offense to entangle me in private financial matters."

"But just because you are a respected person, your honor, I must turn to you. I have no family left alive."

So, heaving a great sigh, the judge agreed.

"I do not wish to disappoint you," he said, "but just to make sure everything is quite proper, kindly have the bag sealed."

"Yes," smiled the old woman. "I have done so."

"Very well then. Go in peace."

It was three years before the old woman completed her journey across the Arabian sea, over the burning sands of the Hejaz[26], to the somber Ka'aba[27], the Well of Zamzam[28], and home again. When she received her pouch from the judge's hands, she knelt in gratitude and said:

"Sir, do me the honor of accepting ten of these gold coins for yourself. The trouble you have taken has allowed me to make my pilgrimage in peace."

"No, no," the judge said quickly. "Just inspect the seal. Are you satisfied that it is intact?"

"Of course," she smiled. "And God bless your honor."

"Go in peace," he murmured.

But when she opened her bag in her small home, the old woman was shocked. Copper coins had been substituted for all her coins of gold! She hobbled back to the magistrate as quickly as her legs would take her, but her story sent him into a towering rage.

"How dare you try to swindle me! All I know is you gave me a sealed bag, and I gave you a sealed bag back. What was in the pouch I haven't the slightest idea. And to think I never even wanted to touch your silly purse in the first place! What impudence! What ingratitude!"

The old woman was desperate.

But fortunately for her, the Emperor was visiting Delhi at that time with all his entourage—including Wazir Birbal.

When Akbar and Birbal heard the complaint, Birbal asked to inspect her money bag. "If the seal really was intact . . ." he mused. And then he had a hunch.

That night, on Birbal's instructions, the King secretly tore a corner of his bed sheet.

The next night when he went to bed he examined the sheet. So cleverly had it been darned that no one ever could have suspected it had been ripped. Calling his valet, he demanded an explanation.

"*Jahanpanah*," quavered the servant, "thinking I had perhaps torn the sheet through carelessness, I was afraid of being punished. So I made inquiries and found the cleverest tailor in the city."

"Tomorrow," smiled Akbar, "he is commanded to come to *durbar.*"

Tailors are not generally asked to appear before grandees of the Empire, and this one was dreadfully nervous at the Imperial summons.

"Apparently you were engaged in secret by my valet," scowled the Emperor.

"Y-yes, *M-Maharaj*,—but I s-saw no h-harm . . ."

"I shall be the judge of that!" thundered the King. "Now who else has hired you in secret—on pain of death!"

"*H-Huzur*," stammered the tailor, "p-people do n-not usually h-hire me in . . . in secret—but I did do one other s-secret job . . ." He paused, for his throat was dry as sand.

"Yes, yes," said Akbar impatiently. "Who for?"

"The J-judge of Delhi," gulped the tailor. "I darned a bag con— containing c-copper coins."

"Let the judge be brought," shouted the King. The judge soon appeared before the Throne. When he saw the tailor at court, his heart failed him.

"Put him under the lash," said Birbal loftily, "in order to loosen his tongue."

"No, no, sir," wailed the judge. "*Jahanpanah*, I confess. I cut the bag—substituted copper for this woman's gold—and had the tailor repair the bag so no one could detect the crime."

Akbar was enraged.

"You are dismissed from your Imperial office in disgrace. Whatever is left of your property after repaying this devout old woman will be distributed to the poor. In your long and ignoble career, I have little doubt you wrenched the wealth you possess from the very people you were appointed to protect."

And the great men of Akbar's Empire trembled and ever remembered the King's swift judgment on an official tempted to cheat the weak and poor.

THE MILK POND

The campaign against the mighty fortress of Chitor, though spectacular and triumphant, was very costly, and Akbar spoke with his ministers about how to pay the expense.

"Tax the people for it," most of them said.

But the Great Mughal was reluctant.

"The glory of the King is something villagers take pride in," said Akbar, "so long as they do not have to pay for it with their daily bread."

"Nonsense," scoffed one of Akbar's commanders. "The Emperor's orders are sacred—the people must obey without hesitation."

"I think the people will find a way to disobey an unjust order," said Birbal.

"Impossible," said the commander.

"Can we test this?" smiled the King.

"Certainly," replied Birbal. "Let us choose a small village. Send this commander to tell every inhabitant to throw a pitcher of milk into the village pond tonight. Tomorrow you and I shall visit the place in disguise."

This suggestion was carried out, and when Akbar and Birbal arrived in the village, on foot and in the guise of religious pilgrims, the King was astonished to see that the village pond was sapphire blue—not a drop of milk in it.

Calling at the home of the village headman, the disguised friends were invited to a meal of yogurt and rice and lentil curry. When they had finished, Akbar turned to their host and said:

"We are travelers from Qandahar, friend, and we find the customs of your country very strange."

"How so, brother?" asked the headman.

"We heard in the bazaar that your King ordered every person in this village to pour a pitcher of milk into the pond last night. Why should your King want a pond full of milk?"

"I do not know the reason," said the headman proudly, "but I am sure he had a good one."

"That is easy for you to say," observed Birbal, "for you are the headman here and could afford to waste a pitcher of milk. But it must have been very hard on the poor."

"This village is not as rich as Delhi," said the crafty headman. "It was just as hard on me as on the poor."

"Are you saying you hesitated to obey the King's command?" asked Akbar.

"No, that would have been an offense . . ."

"So what did you do?" asked Birbal.

"Well," said the headman, leaning forward with a wink, "to be quite honest, I did not obey it at all. Instead of milk, I poured a jug of water into the pond—with the milk of all the others, how could a single pitcher be missed?"

Akbar and Birbal traded smiles, realizing now why the pond was still crystal clear. Every villager had shirked the order, thinking all his neighbors would obey!

Now, while Akbar was ready to accept this lesson, the commander who had given the villagers the order was outraged.

"That headman and everyone in his village must be punished for defying an Imperial Command," he cried. "Otherwise no one will bother to obey Your Majesty—and perhaps one day the people's obedience may be a matter of life and death!"

The other courtiers agreed.

Akbar saw he would have to give in. Then Birbal intervened:

"If the headman must be punished, bring him to court. But let me at least choose the people who will decide his punishment."

"You are my Wazir," said Akbar, "and that is your privilege."

So, while the commander dragged the terrified headman to the Imperial *Diwan*, Birbal scoured the bazaars of Fatehpur Sikri for the five poorest beggars in the city.

"I am displeased with this man," said Akbar to the beggar's jury and pointed a bejeweled finger at the guilty man. "He has hoarded a pitcher of milk from the Crown. You will decide a punishment to fit his crime."

When they had withdrawn to a private chamber, the beggars consulted each other.

"We shall be punished if we do not give a harsh enough sentence," said the first. "For disobeying the King we could have him executed."

"Oh, no," said the second. "That is far too cruel. Let us send him into exile."

"What about his family?" said the third. "How will they live if he is gone? The best solution is to fine him."

"Let us fine him heavily," said the fourth. "Two hundred rupees."

"Two hundred rupees!" cried the fifth. "It would take years to beg for so much. Let it be a hundred."

"Even that would take months to collect," said the first. "How will he manage? Let it be ten."

And since none of them had ever seen as much as ten rupees at a time, the beggar's jury settled on this punishment.

When Akbar heard the sentence, he thanked the beggars and sent them away with precious gifts. Then Birbal demanded the small sum from the headman, who paid it, greatly relieved that he was not to lose his head.

"The sentence certainly would not have been the same," remarked Birbal, "if the crime of hoarding a single pitcher of milk had been judged by the wealthiest nobles of the realm."

"And the tax for our latest victories in battle shall be paid from my private treasure," said the Emperor, "for, after all, the Fortress of Chitor is now mine."

The Queen Is Punished

A kbar was very displeased with his son, Prince Salim.

"What is the matter with you?" he asked Jodh Bai, the Queen. "Don't you take any interest in his studies? Look how badly he has failed all his examinations, even though the most distinguished mathematicians and philosophers are his tutors."

"He is still a boy," said the Queen mildly.

"A boy!" puffed Akbar. "When I was his age, I could answer all the scholars' questions. I may not have learned to read and write, but look how far I have come today."

"Well," the Queen continued, "Your mother tells me that when you were Salim's age, you were exactly like your grandfather—only interested in hunting, pigeon-flying, and polo."

"If that is the sort of answer you give me when I am speaking about the welfare of our son, I doubt whether you are fit to be Queen!" shouted the King. "Pack your things and return to your father's house. I do not want you here any longer."

Stunned, Jodh Bai fell at Akbar's feet.

"Refuge of the World, Sun of My Life—how can I live without you?"

The *Begum's* tears made Akbar feel a little softer, but he still refused to give in. Lifting her up, he said:

"You may take with you any object from the palace which is dear to you when you leave."

And he left her with her servants to pack.

Just at this moment, Birbal happened to present himself at the Queen's apartments to pay his respects—something he was careful to do at least weekly after Jodh Bai and her brother had plotted against him.

"Ah, the King's best friend," cried the Queen to Birbal acidly. "Perhaps you are the one filling his head with such stubborn ideas."

"Your Radiant Highness knows that I am the King's humble servant," said Birbal, bowing. "It is not for me to give orders, but to carry out his august commands."

"Humph!" sniffed the Queen. "You know how to get yourself out of trouble, that's certain. Well, maybe this time you can help *me.*"

"I would be honored to learn how I may serve," purred Birbal.

So the Queen sat next to Birbal, wrapping her hands around her knees like a schoolgirl, and told the whole story of the King's unjust wrath. When she had finished, Birbal said:

"I'm afraid if he has ordered it, you will have to go. But," he continued, rubbing his chin, "he did say you could take with you whatever you held dear . . ."

"Yes," the Queen agreed.

"So," said Birbal, "here is what you must do . . ."

And following Birbal's instructions, the *Begum* ordered her servants to pack all her jewelry and clothing in fragrant sandalwood chests. When all was ready, she sent a message to the King:

"Do not deny me the light of your eyes before I bid farewell to the palace forever."

Frowning, Akbar went to the Queen's apartments to say good-bye. He was always very touched by her beauty in sadness or in anger, and he steeled himself in case she pleaded for forgiveness again. But all she said was:

"Will you allow me to serve Your Highness one last glass of *julab*[29] before I leave?"

"I have no objection," said Akbar, gruffly.

But hardly had he tasted the rose-scented drink, than the veil of drowsiness drifted over his eyes. He sank at once into the deepest sleep.

The Queen sprung into action. Swiftly ordering her servants, she had the Emperor loaded into a silk-lined palanquin and carried, along with everything she owned, through the gates of Fatehpur Sikri to her father's city of Amber, many miles away.

The drug in the *julab* did not wear off for two days. When the Emperor woke at last he found the Queen at his bedside.

"Where am I?" he thundered. "This is your father's house! How did I get here? Treason!"

But Jodh Bai took his hand.

"Refuge of the World, you told me when I was leaving the palace that I could take with me the one thing I loved best. The people may live without an Emperor, but my heart cannot live without its King."

Akbar was touched by her answer, and he took his beautiful wife in his arms.

"Let us find a way to deprive neither the people nor your heart—return with me to the palace," he smiled.

And when Birbal next paid his respects to the *Begum* in her apartments, he was rewarded with a chest of luminous gems.

EGGPLANTS

One fine day, after lunch, as Akbar and Birbal sat watching the silver whirlpools in the river, the Emperor began to rhapsodize about the eggplant. He called it the most delicious, beautifully purple, and nutritious vegetable in the world. He confided that even as a young prince he had been devoted to eggplants.

Birbal not only agreed; he even improvised an Ode to Eggplants. Akbar was delighted.

Word filtered down to the Imperial Chef, who naturally began to think up all kinds of new and exotic recipes for eggplants. For the next several days, eggplants featured prominently on the royal menu.

At first, Akbar was pleased. But soon the novelty wore off. One week later, when the Birbal and the King were lunching on the terrace, the servants laid an elaborate eggplant curry before them.

"Eggplants again?" snapped Akbar. "Eggplants are the most worthless, vile, despicable vegetables ever grown. Give them to Birbal. He loves eggplants!"

"On the contrary, Sire," said Birbal, "I enjoy eggplants about as much as I do a splinter. I think if I never saw another eggplant in my life, I might die happy."

Akbar lost all patience. "A week ago," he reminded him, "you agreed with me that the eggplant was the noblest food in existence. You even *sang* its praises!"

"Ah, but Sire," explained Birbal. "I serve the Emperor, not the vegetable."

THE RUG MERCHANT

One day a rug merchant from Kashmir came into the Hall of Public Audience at Agra. His turban was torn, and his eyes were bleary with care.

"I am lost! I am ruined! Please help me, Great King!"

"What is all this?" growled Akbar. "Who let him in?"

"Please, O Shadow of God Upon the Earth! Only you can give me justice."

"Very well," sighed Akbar. "Let us hear your case."

"Sire," said the merchant. "I hired a boat to carry my cargo of fine carpets from Kashmir. But when I reached the landing, the boatman and his crew threw me ashore without my carpets. Now he claims my cargo belongs to him."

The Emperor turned to Birbal. "Bring the boatman and his crew. We shall hear the other side."

Birbal went to the banks of the Jumna and found the skipper. Two burly guards escorted him and his crew to the Palace.

"This Kashmiri is lying," said the boatman. "The goods belong to me. You may ask any member of my crew."

"Well?" said Birbal.

One of the shabby oarsmen stepped forward. "Our *Sahib* speaks the truth, sir. This Kashmiri was just a passenger. He was drunk the whole journey. Then he claimed he had no money to pay his passage. We threw him ashore, and now he says our *Sahib's* goods are his."

"Do you all agree with this report?" Birbal asked the other sailors. All nodded yes.

Birbal paused, stroking his chin. Then he said:

"Return tomorrow. We shall settle the argument then."

That evening Birbal and a friend disguised themselves as wealthy merchants and went strolling down the riverbank. After a while, they found the boatman's craft.

"*Namaste*[30]," cried Birbal.

"*Salaam*," replied the boatman.

"Have you any goods to sell?" asked Birbal.

"Ah, good sir, I have the finest carpets of Kashmir."

"What are you asking?" Birbal queried.

"A thousand gold *mohurs*," said the boatman. "They are carpets fit for the court of the King."

"Indeed," Birbal yawned. "Well, the carpet market is very bad in Agra these days." And, turning to his friend, Birbal said, "Clerk, look at the goods and tell me what they are worth."

So Birbal's friend went with the boatman and unrolled the carpets upon the dock. He looked at the back, counted the knots, and viewed them from every side.

"Not very good," he said. "The pile is thin, not evenly cut, and the designs are nothing special. Even if they were Persian, I would not pay more than five hundred gold coins . . ."

"Half my price?" gulped the oarsman.

"But as they are Kashmiri and very inferior," he continued, "three hundred is as high as you should go."

"Well, my good man," said Birbal. "There you have it. Three hundred is my highest offer."

The boatman scratched his head. "It doesn't seem fair," he gulped. "But if that's the best you can do, I'll have to swallow my pride."

"Sold, then," said Birbal. "We shall come in the morning to do the deal."

"Peace upon you," sighed the boatman.

"And upon you peace," smiled Birbal.

Now Birbal and his friend went to a nearby inn and made inquiries after the Kashmiri merchant. They found him, drowning his sorrows in *arrack*[31].

"I hear you have brought carpets to sell in the city," said the disguised Birbal. The Kashmiri brightened up.

"They are as fine as any from Persia," he replied.

"How much?" asked Birbal, stifling a yawn.

"A thousand gold *mohurs*," said the Kashmiri. "It is a fair price."

"Well, the demand for carpets is very bad nowadays," said Birbal. "I'll give you five hundred. Take it or leave it."

"Five hundred!" shouted the Kashmiri, jumping up. "Is everyone in this city a thief? One thousand is a fairer price than you'll ever find for carpets of that quality and design!"

"Very well," said the merchant. "Let's settle on seven hundred."

"One thousand is a just price," cried the Kashmiri, "and I'll never take a copper less."

"Friend," smiled the disguised Birbal, "no one in Agra will pay one thousand coins. Think again."

"I've done a lot of thinking since I came to this accursed place," shouted the Kashmiri. "I'll take them all the way back to Kashmir before I'll sell them for less than a thousand. It is a fair and proper price!"

"Have it your way," shrugged Birbal. And he and his friend went their way.

The next day in *durbar*, Birbal called one of the scrawny sailors before the throne.

"I know the truth," said Birbal, "and so do you. I will give you one last chance to come clean. Tell me who is lying, the Kashmiri or your *Sahib*. If you are honest, you shall go free with a reward. If you lie, you and all the other sailors shall lose your heads. Now speak!"

The oarsman collapsed on his knees.

"Please, sir, I am a poor man. I was afraid of my *Sahib*. He paid me twenty coppers to lie. The goods belong to the Kashmiri. Please forgive me."

"But this is absurd!" cried the boatman.

"Silence!" called Birbal. And then he explained how he and his friend had tested the matter in disguise.

"A thief will cheaply part with stolen good," he said, "but an upright man takes pride in the value of his honest toil."

The Emperor rose from his throne in anger. "You," he thundered to the boatman, "shall get fifty lashes and a thousand *mohur* fine. For every coin you cannot pay, you shall spend a month in jail. And to you, dear friend from Kashmir, my Treasurer shall pay the thousand coins for each of your carpets, and you may henceforward say you are purveyor of Kashmiri carpets to the King."

Birbal's House

Once a man came from the country to consult Birbal on some urgent matter. Having reached the street where the Wazir lived, he wandered fretfully up and down, hoping to catch sight of someone who could guide him aright.

He was so distracted that he collided smack into a man who was himself hurrying out from one of the houses. When the two had risen from the ground and were dusting themselves off, the yokel exclaimed:

"Brother, I must know immediately which is the house of Wazir Birbal!"

"That one," said the man, pointing, and hastened on his way.

The man lingered in front of the house and made inquiries of the gardeners, but they told him that Wazir Birbal had gone to *durbar* and would not return for some time.

There was nothing to do but prop himself against the gate and wait in the stinging dust of the busy street and the coppery heat of the Indian sun.

When late in the evening he saw a man approach and go straight through the gate as if he were the owner, he was astonished to recognize the same man he had bumped into that morning.

"*Huzur,*" cried the villager, "when I met you earlier in this very lane, why did you not tell me then that you yourself were Wazir Birbal?"

"Friend," smiled Birbal, "when you asked for my house, I showed you my house. If you had asked for me, I would have told you Birbal was standing before you. You were in such a hurry to get the information you wanted, you would never have listened to the advice you need. Now, come."

And Birbal escorted the weary villager into his home.

GOOD NEWS AND BAD NEWS

Not everybody who came to Birbal for advice really needed it. Consulting the sage friend of the King had become something of a fashion.

One day a rich neighbor came to the Wazir's house and said:

"I am desperately unhappy. The finest Arabian mare in my stables ran away a week ago. At first I hoped someone might return her, but she is nowhere to be found."

Birbal, reclining on silken cushions, stifled a yawn.

"It could have been worse," he said lazily.

The old man was annoyed and went away, grumbling.

But the following morning his horse returned, together with a wild stallion of beautiful proportions, worth even more than the wandering mare. The old man hurried back to Birbal to express his delight. But Birbal scarcely looked up from a book he was reading as he murmured:

"I foresee trouble."

Even more irritated than before, the neighbor stormed off.

But that afternoon the old man's son tried to ride the wild stallion, was thrown, and broke his leg. Passing by Birbal's verandah on the way to the hospital, the old man shouted:

"See what your accursed pessimism has done to my boy, Birbal? Now he may be a cripple for life!"

But Birbal, who was sipping a cool *julab*, replied:

"Good may come of it."

Furious, the old man marched off, telling everyone in his path that Birbal had gone out of his mind.

The very next day a royal edict went out, calling all able-bodied young men to report for soldier's duty, as a new war had erupted on the Afghan Frontier. All across the Empire, parents wept as their sons set forth, for they knew they might never see them again. But the old man's son, being in the hospital, was excused from serving in the army.

Gratefully, he hurried to the house of Birbal, whom he found tending the roses in his cool garden. But before he could blurt out his thanks, Birbal silenced him by holding up his hand and said:

"People like you believe in luck—but unfortunately you are only able to think about one part of life at a time. Try to remember, my friend: when your house burns down—at least you get revenge upon the bedbugs!"

LIFE

A kbar was listening to an old soldier, who, as a boy, had accompanied
the first Mughal Emperor, Babur, on his conquest of Hindustan.
"When your father was only twenty-three, *Jahanpanah*, he fell deathly
ill. Sitting on the banks of the River Jumna, your grandfather, Babur, asked
his wise men what to do. They said Humayun would live if Babur would

give away the most precious thing he owned. They were greedy men and meant the fabulous *Koh-i-Nur* diamond—the 'Mountain of Light.' But Babur understood this to mean his life.

"Three times he walked around Humayun's bed, crying aloud his heartfelt offer to God—his life for the boy's. No sooner had the prayers escaped his lips than the boy began to recover—while Babur caught fever and soon died.

"Shah Babur is remembered not only as the finest warrior of his age, but as a poet and a loving father."

There was respectful silence as the old soldier ended his tale. Then, suddenly, little Prince Salim came running into the Royal Audience Hall and climbed onto the Emperor's lap. Normally, for this unruliness, he would have been punished, but now Akbar folded the cooing child into his arms.

"Is there anything dearer in the world," asked Akbar, "than the life of a child to its parent?"

"Certainly not, *Huzur*," murmured various courtiers with respect.

But Birbal said not a word.

"Birbal?" asked the King, puzzled. "Do you have a different opinion?"

"It is not my opinion, *Jahanpanah*, but a fact. One's own life is dearer than the life of one's child—even your grandfather thought so, for in sacrificing his most precious possession, it was his *own* life he offered, not Humayun's."

"You are twisting the story," said the Emperor. "Can you prove what you say?"

"Yes, *Maharaj*, with some of your gardeners' assistance."

So Akbar and his retinue followed Birbal to the garden. Birbal found a small lotus tank and had a gardener empty it. Then Birbal ordered another gardener to catch one of the many gray apes which always roamed the rooftops of the city.

"But," he specified, "it must be a mother monkey with babies."

This was an adventure in itself, but under the watchful eyes of the Emperor, the hapless gardeners managed to capture a hissing and scolding mother monkey and twins, presenting them just as the lotus tank was completely drained.

"Now," said Birbal. "Place the monkeys inside the tank, and fill it again."

The King and all his courtiers peered over the edge, fascinated.

When the mother monkey found the water in the pond rising, she took her babies on her back to save them from drowning. When the water began to lap around her chest, she stood straight up and made her young sit on her head.

"Do you see, Birbal?" asked the King. "Her first thought is for her children."

"The pond is not yet full," replied Birbal.

Soon the water reached the mother's mouth. With a scream, she jumped out of the pond, leaving her young ones behind.

Birbal immediately told one of the miserable gardeners to leap into the tank and save the baby monkeys—and, of course, under the Emperor's gaze, he did it.

When the mother monkey had scooped up her young and sprung indignantly into a nearby tree, Birbal turned to Akbar and said:

"Our children are dear to us indeed, but the dearest thing in the world is one's own life, a gift directly from the hand of God. You have just seen, *Maharaj*, the proof of it."

THE SUIT OF ARMOR

A famous metal worker of Lucknow made a superb suit of armor and brought it to the Emperor on campaign.

"Let us test its strength," said the Mughal.

Laying the armor on the ground, Akbar summoned his mightiest war elephant and had it step on the breastplate, which flattened like a leaf.

"No good," remarked the King.

The metal smith was crestfallen, but he patiently pried up the armor platter, which represented his savings of many months, and headed home.

Birbal felt sorry for him and met him at the edge of camp. Handing him some money, he said: "Try again."

Gratefully, the artisan hammered out the strongest and most comely suit of armor that Lucknow had ever seen. Then he returned to the Emperor's pavilion and presented it to Akbar.

Calling for his war elephant, the King said:

"Let us try again."

But Birbal intervened.

"*Jahanpanah*, I think it is a fairer test if somebody is in the armor—I'll volunteer."

"But that is the point of the test," said Akbar, "to learn the worst before someone trusts this armor with his life."

"Still," said Birbal, "I would like to try."

"As you wish," shrugged the King.

But when Birbal lay down, clad in the armor, the elephant refused to step on him—for this was Akbar's famous "Judgment Elephant"—so wise he would never trample an innocent man, even if a judge had wrongly found him guilty. The elephant merely nudged Birbal with his trunk.

So Birbal rose and said:

"Let the executioner try the armor with his sword."

So the royal executioner swung at Birbal with a flashing scimitar—but with a deft maneuver, Birbal avoided the blow, tripped the executioner, and sent him sprawling.

"Well," drawled the King. "This is all very amusing, but I don't see what it tells us about the armor."

"Ah, but *Huzur*," echoed Birbal from deep inside the helmet. "When a King wins in battle, the people set *him* upon the throne—not his suit of armor. Victory owes something to the wearer. A fool or a coward, even in armor as hard as diamond, would quickly perish in war."

Akbar laughed.

"Very well. Let the metal smith from Lucknow be rewarded, for if God preserves my right arm, the armor will prove strong enough. And if God preserves Birbal as my Wazir, we shall perhaps need fewer wars."

A Child's Whim

One day, after a long day dealing with an irritating ambassador from the Shah of Persia, Akbar entered his private apartments, exhausted.

Prince Salim, who was still just a boy, ran up to the King and jumped in his lap.

"Father, will you give me sugar cane?"

Smiling wearily, Akbar called a servant and gave the order. Sugar cane, cut into short segments, was brought in a beautiful dish.

"Why did you cut it up, Father? I didn't want it cut up. I wanted a whole one."

"Very well," grumbled Akbar. "Bring him a whole one."

But before the servant could leave, the child shouted:

"No, I don't want *another* whole one! I want *that* one—but not cut up!"

"Now, look here," said Akbar. "Your mother may spoil you—"

But Prince Salim started to cry so loudly, Akbar gave in.

"All right, all right. Why don't you take something else, eh? Be a good boy. Be a *quiet* boy, and I'll give you anything you like."

With these words, Salim stopped crying and snatched a priceless ruby from Akbar's turban.

"This is pretty," said the child. But no sooner had he snatched it than he pricked himself on its mounting pin. The gem fell from his tiny fingers, rolled off the verandah, and into the moat.

"That did it!" shouted Akbar. "That ruby was one of the finest of Badakhshan,[32] given to me by my father! Now you are going to be punished."

But at that moment the Queen walked in, and little Salim darted behind her skirts.

"Do you know what your spoiled son has done now?" said Akbar. And he angrily explained.

"He's only a child," said the Queen, stroking Salim's hair.

"Nonsense!" said the King. "He is a prince. If I had done such a thing at his age, my father would have—anyway, he must take the consequences!"

"Well," said the Queen, petting Salim's hair, "if you insist on punishing him, promise me you will not do it until tomorrow. Then at least you will punish him justly and not out of anger."

Akbar grumbled. "I don't know why I always let you talk me into things. I'm King in half the world, but not in my own home." Still, he relented.

That night the Queen sent a message to Birbal, explaining Akbar's harsh manner with his son. Birbal thought a bit and sent his servants to the bazaar. On Birbal's orders, they hired a snake charmer who had a cobra in a basket with its mouth sewn shut.

The next morning, as the King took an early walk in his garden, Birbal led little Salim by the hand to a place beside a fountain where the snake charmer was sitting. The snake charmer took the lid off his basket and began to rock and play his flute, and the cobra spread its hood and rose up, swaying.

When the little boy saw this curious creature, he dashed forward, trying to grasp it in his hands. Seeing this, Akbar ran toward the Prince.

"Birbal, are you mad?" shouted the King, sweeping the child from harm's way. "How can you stand there like an idiot and allow him to reach for a cobra?"

"What's the matter?" asked Birbal. "If he's old enough to know the value of a ruby, he is surely old enough to know the danger of a snake. He must take the consequences."

At these words Akbar looked closely at the cobra, saw his mouth was sewn shut, and realized this was but another of Birbal's graphic lessons. Holding the Prince up to his face, the Emperor said:

"Salim—this Uncle Birbal of yours has saved your skin. I only hope you will be as merciful as he, when one day you sit on the Peacock Throne."

Horse Sense

Akbar, like any sensible King of his day, kept spies at the courts of neighboring princes, so that he would know in advance if they planned to attack his vast Empire of Hindustan.

One of these spies from the court of the Persian Shah had a vital message for the Emperor. Being on a secret mission, he made the long ride from Ispahan to Fatehpur Sikri alone. He needed to travel too quickly to join a lumbering merchant caravan for protection, and he did not want a military escort, for fear it would attract attention.

But when he neared the Imperial Capital, he began to relax, and, cantering along, he noticed a traveler by the wayside who looked forlorn.

"Good fellow," called the spy. "Where are you from?"

"Bikaner[33], friend. But I have been robbed of my horse and money . . ."

"Here, brother," said the emissary of the King. "Ride behind me, and I will find you lodging when we reach the city."

"May your life be long!" exclaimed the traveler, leaping up behind the spy.

When at last they reached the Palace gate, the spy slipped from his horse and offered to help the traveler down from the saddle. But the traveler did not budge.

"Why should I get down?" asked the traveler, who was really a clever thief. "I have given you a lift, haven't I? Be on your way."

"What!" shouted the spy. "That's my horse!"

"*Your* horse? Really, this fellow is too good," laughed the thief, looking at the people who had begun to gather around. "I give him a ride, and *he* wants to keep the horse. This is an ungrateful world."

In hot fury, the spy lunged at the thief and knocked him to the ground. They struggled until two palace guards ran forward and pulled them apart.

As luck would have it, the Palace gate flew open at just that moment, and the Emperor, with Birbal at his side, rode out.

"What is the meaning of this?" thundered the King, glancing at the scuffle. The situation was quickly explained. Akbar rubbed his chin.

"I have it," he mused. "We shall set the two men apart at a hundred paces and let the horse decide. Whichever man the horse follows must be its master."

Birbal laughed.

"I take it," said Akbar dryly, "the Wazir objects?"

"O Star of Bright Promise," laughed Birbal. "Suppose the owner of the horse has ridden it hard over a long journey, as, from the mud and sweat on the animal, I would say he has. If the horse has any sense, he will go to the other man, to try his luck with a new master. If, on the other hand, the horse has no sense, what good is such a test?"

"Ah, very well," grinned Akbar. "You be the judge."

"Let me have the horse," Birbal told the men. "Present yourselves at the Royal Stables tomorrow morning."

When morning came, the thief and the spy presented themselves to the King, Birbal, and a mixed bag of curious nobles. Birbal led them to the stalls where the Royal horses were kept. There were well over a thousand beautiful steeds.

"All I ask is that you claim the horse which belongs to you. Which of you wishes to go first?"

"I do," cried the spy, eagerly.

"Then you shall go second," said Birbal. And he prodded the thief forward.

But the thief hesitated miserably. How could he possibly pick one horse from a thousand—especially when he had only ridden him once? After making several false starts and then halting, unsure, Birbal growled:

"You are wasting His Majesty's precious time. You!" He pointed to the spy. "Take your turn."

The spy walked straight to his horse and led it from its stall.

Thus was the thief punished and the spy chastised—for Akbar tolerated no diversion when an officer was on the service of the King.

An Endless Tale

Akbar was an inexhaustible worker at the trade of King and was accustomed to sleeping only three hours a night. When he fell sick and his doctors insisted that he stay in bed, he found it very difficult to give up his usually energetic routine. His physicians gave him sleeping potions, but nothing helped his restlessness.

At last the chief medic said:

"If you don't relax, you won't get better. What you need is something to soothe your mind. I suggest Your Majesty should hear a story every night before retiring, so that your thoughts may be cheerful and dreamy. Then you will sleep peacefully."

"Good idea," said the King, who adored stories. "But how shall I get a man to tell me a different story every night?"

"You have a court full of noblemen, *Jahanpanah*. Surely each of them, in turn, could tell you a different story every night."

The royal command went out, and each evening a courtier presented himself at the King's bed chamber to spin a yarn.

But this became a real problem for the courtiers. In the first place, each would have to make sure that his story had not been told by somebody before him, because if he showed up with only one tale and the Emperor had already heard it, he was sure to earn Akbar's displeasure. Second, every time the courtiers *did* manage to tell the Emperor a story, at the end of it, the restless Akbar would always ask:

"What next?"

So the noblemen had to add another tale to the first, and then another story to that, and so on. And this went on until the story teller, not the listener, began to nod asleep.

Fearing to lose their heads if they should commit the unpardonable sin of dozing in the Imperial Presence, the courtiers finally consulted Birbal. The Wazir laughed.

"Who is up for telling the story tonight?" asked Birbal.

"I am," said a miserable courtier, Hussein Khan.

"Will you let me take your place?"

Hussein Khan brightened.

"A thousand thanks, brother!" he cried. "I will pay you to take it!"

"Never mind that," smiled Birbal. "Let us see what I can do."

The Emperor welcomed Birbal, and settled in for a good tale. Birbal wove a fable as only his eloquent wit could do, carrying the King's imagination on a magic carpet of words. But when the story ended, the Emperor came down out of the clouds and noticed Birbal rising to leave.

"Just a moment, Birbal—what happened then?"

So Birbal settled himself once again upon a cushion and spun another tale of adventure, romance, and intrigue, with many twists and turns in the plot, going on for about an hour. But, as soon as it was over, Akbar launched the same royal question:

"What next?"

So it went with the third story, whose final sentence had hardly escaped Birbal's lips, when the King's words tickled his ears:

"What next?"

Smiling, Birbal began his next story in this way:

"Once upon a time, in the remotest jungle in the farthest South, there lived a tribesman in a hut made of sticks and mud."

"Yes, yes . . ." said Akbar eagerly.

"The jungle was home to a thousand birds and beasts, from towering elephants who thundered through the underbrush, to supple panthers with golden eyes, to sly jackals and lordly tigers . . ."

"Yes . . ."

"Well, the tribesman knew how to protect himself from beasts, for, strong as they were, none dared approach the little hut with its smoldering fire—for the beasts were terrified of fire."

"Yes . . ."

"But the tribesman had a problem with the birds. No matter how he tried to protect his store of grain, they always managed to flit into his hut and come out again, carrying in their beaks his precious kernels of corn."

"Yes . . ."

"So he thought and he thought, and in the end he wove a large basket, put his grain inside, and tied a lid tightly on top."

"Yes, what next?"

"When the birds, as usual, entered the hut, they could not find food anywhere, and they turned their attention to the basket."

"What happened then?"

"The birds pecked at the basket, but it was too tightly woven by the wily tribal for them to cut a hole. They only hurt themselves trying."

"What then?"

"Among the birds was a clever sparrow. When the others were ready to give up, she made friends with a tiny field mouse, who agreed to nibble a hole in the basket for his share of the tribesman's grain."

"Yes . . ."

"The word spread quickly among the birds of the jungle, and soon the air was filled with chirping and the drumming of wings. Five hundred of them crowded around the old man's hut."

"So many!" exclaimed the King. "What then?"

"Well," smiled Birbal, "one bird flew into the hut, seized a grain of corn in its beak, and flew out."

"Then?"

"Then a second bird flew into the hut, seized a grain of corn in *its* beak, and flew out."

"Hm. Then?"

"Well, then the third bird flew into the hut, seized a grain of corn in *its* beak, and flew out."

"Yes, yes, but what then?"

"Then a fourth bird flew into the hut, seized a grain of corn in *its* beak, and flew out."

"I get the point, Birbal, but what happened after that?"

"Well, after that, *Huzur*, a *fifth* bird flew into the hut, seized a grain of corn in *its* beak, and—"

"Birbal," asked the King sitting up in his bed, "just how many of these birds have we got left?"

"*Maharaj*, only five birds have received their grain. That leaves four hundred and ninety-five birds impatiently waiting, not to mention the cousins and in-laws of the field mouse. But, as I was saying, the *sixth* bird then sailed into the old man's cottage, seized a grain of corn in its beak, and—"

"Just a moment!" shouted the Emperor, holding his hand up in disgust. "When are these stupid birds going to finish the job and carry off all of the grain?"

"*Jahanpanah*, probably when you stop asking 'What next?'"

Akbar leaned back against his pillow, reflected, and then chuckled:

"Very well, Birbal. You may tell the courtiers that their story-telling duties are over. And you may take the birds and field mice with you as you go."

THE SWORD OF ADVERSITY

One day, as Akbar and Birbal strolled among the chattering fountains of the Imperial garden, the King pondered aloud: "Why are my noblemen so eternally jealous? They have more than most of humanity put together. Why do they always plot one against another?"

Smiling, Birbal replied, "Because the poor make merry on what they gain by their wit, while the nobles spend their lives fretting that they will lose what has been handed down to them for nothing."

"Can you show me?" asked Akbar.

"Hearing is obedience, O Peacock of the Age."

That evening, Birbal took the King disguised into the streets of Fatehpur Sikri. Dressed as poor men, they visited the home of a humble shoemaker.

Although it was a moonless night, and although they were strangers, the shoemaker welcomed them into his meager home. The shoemaker and his family played musical instruments, sang, and produced the best feast in their power. Akbar was surprised. He did not receive as joyful a welcome in some of the noblest houses of his realm.

"Surely," said Akbar to Birbal on the way home, "circumstances alter cases. I mean, he would not be so jolly if disaster struck."

"Well," said Birbal, "possibly not. But, Sire, the poor learn that you are about as happy as you make up your mind to be."

Akbar resolved to test the shoemaker's resilience. So he decreed that all shoemaking in the city must cease on pain of death.

When the shoemaker learned of this, he thought: "How shall I make a living?" The sweat rolled off his neck. Noticing the heat, he thought, "I shall get ice and sell cold water in the streets." And doing so, he earned more on that hot afternoon than he ever had made selling shoes.

That night, the disguised King and Birbal visited the shoemaker again. The family's feast and merriment were greater than before. Answering Akbar's puzzled inquiries, the man explained how he obeyed the King's command and had discovered even greater opportunity through that apparent hardship. Birbal smiled.

But the next day Akbar decreed that no water sellers were allowed to ply their trade in Fatehpur Sikri.

The shoemaker pondered what to do next. Standing by the roadside, he noticed a squad of the King's Guards, marching through the city, loudly recruiting troops. The shoemaker volunteered. He received chain mail and a gleaming, razor-sharp sword. But the shoemaker sold the sword at a great profit and replaced it with a wooden one. After all, you couldn't tell the difference with it snug in its scabbard, and in the peace and safety of Akbar's capital, who would ever resort to a sword?

That night the King and Birbal visited the shoemaker again. With the profit of his latest sale, his family was enjoying a bigger party than ever. Shaking his head in disbelief, the King made his usual enquiry. The guard lowered his voice, and, on condition that the mysterious stranger keep it absolutely secret, he explained how he had sold his sword and bought food and drink with the proceeds. Birbal laughed.

But the next day, the King decided to condemn Jai Mal to death. Jai Mal was his bother-in-law, and the King felt that it was generally sound policy to keep all brothers-in-law on the hop. The Emperor summoned the shoemaker and commanded him to carry out the execution. Burly soldiers hauled a quivering Jai Mal into the Imperial Presence.

The shoemaker dropped beads of perspiration. Thinking quickly, he said, "O King, live forever! But this man is innocent."

"Yes!" gurgled Jai Mal.

"He is guilty," frowned the King. "Cut off his head!"

The shoemaker replied, "God's Shadow upon the Earth, I have looked into his eyes, and I know in my soul he is innocent."

"I am," choked Jai Mal feebly.

The Emperor was outraged.

"How dare you quibble with my sentence? Cut off his head, or I will have one of these soldiers lop off yours!"

Gulping, the shoemaker ventured, "Your wish is my command, O Full Moon."

"No!" shrieked Jai Mal.

But then the shoemaker fell to his knees, raised his hands to Heaven, and prayed aloud:

"O Sovereign God, if, as I believe, this man is innocent, turn my sword into wood!"

Then, with a flourish, the shoemaker leapt to his feet, drew his sword, gnashed his teeth, and swung it with a slap across Jai Mal's wincing neck.

To the astonishment of the whole court, Jai Mal survived with nothing but a bruise. The sword was wooden, indeed!

"A miracle!" cried the nobles.

But Akbar could hardly contain his mirth. He commended the shoemaker for his faith and gave him a bag of gold. Then he sent Jai Mal gratefully staggering on his way.

When they were alone, Birbal and the King broke down in torrents of laughter. When they had finished wiping the tears from their eyes, Akbar asked, "Well, my friend, what have we now learned?"

"That the poor man *uses* his head, *Jahanpanah*, while the rich man wastes his life fearing to *lose* it."

THE DONKEY

A Portuguese visitor to the Mughal Court was fond of chewing tobacco—a habit the Emperor despised.

One day Akbar, Birbal, and this Jesuit Father were strolling upon the ramparts of Fatehpur Sikri. The priest rudely spit his tobacco over the parapet. Akbar noticed a donkey grazing in the fields below. Seeing that the donkey nibbled everything except tobacco plants, the King remarked:

"Even a donkey will not chew tobacco."

But rather than take the hint graciously, the Portuguese grew red-faced with anger. Akbar regretted his remark. So Birbal immediately chimed in:

"True, *Huzur*—only a donkey would *not*."

The three smiled together, and, having thus saved face, the Portuguese was careful never again to let his tobacco bother the Emperor at court.

THE PRINCE OF KASHMIR

Akbar, like his father and grandfather before him, coveted the beautiful kingdom of Kashmir, with its cool climate, running streams, and charming gardens. He dreamed a of finding some excuse that would let him conquer it for his Empire.

On one occasion, one of his ministers, Bhagwan Das, made a treaty with Yusuf, the Sultan of Kashmir, who agreed to give all the fragrant mint, precious saffron, silk, and the game of Kashmir's forests to the Mughal Crown—so long as Kashmir remained free. He also invited Yusuf's son, Yuqub, to visit Akbar, promising him that he would return safely home.

Akbar, however, disapproved. He was irritated that his minister should make so important a treaty without asking him, and he flung Yuqub, Prince of Kashmir, into prison.

Now all the courtiers pleaded with Akbar to let Yuqub go.

"This is not like Your Majesty to break a promise."

"*I* made no promise," snapped Akbar. "Bhagwan Das made the promise. And thanks to his idiotic meddling, I may *never* be able to take Kashmir."

"But his promise was made in your name," objected one noble. "And the name of Akbar is famous in all the world for chivalry and honor . . ."

The Emperor scowled. He realized that they were right, but it goaded him to admit that he was wrong. His mood got blacker and blacker. When he saw Birbal enter the *diwan*, he exploded:

"No you don't, Birbal! I know they have brought you here. You want to persuade me to free Yuqub. Well, you may have the sharpest arguments of all the Nine Jewels, but I will not listen to you or to a thousand clever devils like you. Let everyone hereby witness that I, Jalaludin Mohammed Akbar Padshah Ghazi, Emperor of Hindustan, do solemnly swear to execute exactly the opposite of the advice Wazir Birbal has come to give me. So let it be written, so let it be done!"

"Well," said Birbal quietly. "Your proclamation is law, of course—but wouldn't you still like to hear what I was going to recommend?"

"Not really," frowned Akbar. "But as long as you realize that what I have just said *will* stand . . ."

"Of course, *Jahanpanah*," said Birbal. "I was going to suggest that you keep Prince Yuqub in jail, throw away the key, and launch an attack on Srinagar[34]. But if you insist upon doing the opposite . . ." Birbal shrugged. "Well, your word is law."

The courtiers smuggled a smile. Akbar was in a one of the worst moods anyone could remember. The King glared at Birbal, blinked, settled back in his throne, rolled his eyes towards heaven—and then suddenly laughed. And the entire court breathed a sigh of relief.

"Load seven camels with gems and gold and send them with Yuqub back to his father in Kashmir," said Akbar. "And everyone leave me alone, or I will send the lot of you with him!"

THE EMPEROR'S PARROT

A Raja of Southern India sent a beautiful parrot in a silver cage to Akbar. The Great Mughal was delighted. The bird was a clever mimic and soon learned to speak even in Turki, the language of the Imperial family. Akbar personally taught his parrot to whistle, sing and crack jokes, and he was very proud of it. All the children of the palace were allowed to feed it fruit and nuts, and the Emperor often said:

"This bird has more intelligent things to say than the Persian Ambassador."

After a while he entrusted the bird to three servants.

"Your job is to look after my parrot," he told them. "Its health and happiness are on your heads. The person who brings me news of its death will himself be put to death."

Akbar meant to impress on them the importance of their job, but the three servants were a great deal more than impressed.

Their first thought upon waking each morning was whether the parrot had spent a restful night. They would dash to its cage to check. At every meal the thought crossed their minds: "What if something happens to that bird while we are eating?" Their appetite failed, and they hurried to its cage to make sure the parrot had fruit.

But in spite of all their care—or perhaps because of it—the parrot eventually died. The servants were so shocked they could do nothing but stare at the cage, open-mouthed, hoping against hope that soon a feather would stir. While they were in this stupor, Birbal happened by.

When the servants explained their problem, Birbal decided to go to Akbar himself.

"Good morning, Birbal," called the Emperor cheerily.

"*Huzur,*" said Birbal slowly, "It is about your parrot . . ."

"My parrot!" shouted the King. "What has happened to him?"

"The amazing thing is," answered Birbal, "this parrot is so clever, so thoughtful, he has become a mystic—a *yogi*[35]."

"What?" asked the Emperor, astonished.

"Yes, it's true," Birbal said. "Weary of worldly things, this bird has begun a life of meditation. Lying on its back with its eyes calmly shut, it wastes no more time in idle chatter, but concentrates every thought upon the Great Beyond . . ."

"This," said Akbar rising, "I must see."

When he reached the silver cage, he observed the bird for several seconds. Then he turned, disgusted, and said:

"Birbal, people call you clever, and still you can't tell if a bird is dead?"

"Dead, *Jahanpanah?* Surely his mind has transcended this worldly plane."

"Birbal!" shouted the King. "Watch my lips: this parrot is dead!"

"Ah, well, only you may say so," murmured Birbal.

"Why may only I say so?" asked Akbar, annoyed.

"Because," smiled Birbal, "your servants are too attached to their heads!"

At this moment the three servants peered nervously from behind a nearby curtain. Seeing their shivers of fear, the Emperor, shaking his head and laughing, gave each a golden *mohur*—along with the King's pardon.

THE CAGED LION

One day the Emperor Akbar was about to end the morning's Public Audience when an unknown artist prostrated himself before the throne:

"Lord of the Land of Mighty Rivers, allow me to present my handiwork to your illustrious court."

The King sat back in his silk-lined throne, smelling a rose and smiling his approval.

For a few moments the man disappeared. Then he returned, hauling a jewel-encrusted cage of silver which housed a ferocious lion. The courtiers let out a cry of alarm—though many of them were warriors known and dreaded from Bengal to Qandahar.

"Never fear," laughed the artist. "Though this lion is life-like, it is only sample of my work."

"Reward him," commanded Akbar, "for, truly, this man's skill almost shames Nature. At any moment I expect to see this statue's nostrils flare or its eyelids blink. I have seen lions in the forests of Sind[36] look less real."

"Your Majesty honors me," said the artist. "But all the world has heard of the sages who serve the Mughal King, and I should like to test them. So here is my challenge: let your wise ones destroy this sculpted lion— but without touching either it or its cage. If they can do this, I shall give them five hundred coins of flashing gold. If no one can, then each who has tried and failed shall pay the same amount to me."

Upon hearing this, not one stingy courtier stepped forward. Who could possibly even nick—let alone destroy—the statue without touching it? Akbar was displeased.

"Surely one of all my nobles, whose fame spreads like dawn throughout the world, will save the honor of our Mughal realm?"

Wazir Birbal stepped forward and inspected the cage and lion, from every angle, rubbing his chin.

"Let firewood be brought," he said at last.

When bundles of brittle sticks were fetched, Birbal had them laid in a ring around the cage. Then he lit them.

As the flames mounted like so many writhing cobras, to the astonishment of every onlooker, the lion began to vanish like the fragment of a dream. Pressing as near to the cage as the burning embers would allow, they saw that the statue was melting—it had been made of wax!

As servants quenched the fire, the artist embraced Birbal and said:

"Artists create illusion. But the ability to see truth—this talent is rare in the world."

Then he presented Birbal with five hundred gold *mohurs*.

Accepting them, Birbal replied:

"Rarer still, brother, are those who use art to reveal the truth. Accept one thousand gold *mohurs* from me."

"And," smiled Akbar to the artist, "an equal number from the King."

Thus another jewel was fixed in the Mughal Crown, and glory of Akbar grew.

THE FOOLS' TAX

One day the Emperor was thinking.

"Nothing is more costly than foolishness. Yet fools are never made to pay for their mistakes—that burden falls to the rest of humanity. This is unfair."

So he summoned Birbal.

"I have decided to create a new tax—a tax on fools. I will therefore need a list of all the fools on my kingdom. Please arrange it."

So Birbal set out to collect the name of every fool in the Empire. He thought it would be briefer to write the list of wise men, but he did not quibble with the King's command.

Meanwhile, a horse trader from Turkistan arrived at Court and asked to see the Emperor. Akbar had a weakness for fine, pedigreed horses—at any cost. The horse trader paraded an exquisite mare before Akbar.

"I must have that horse!" cried the King.

"Ah, but *Jahanpanah*," said the crafty Turkoman. "This is only one of a hundred such horses I own. Had it not been for the heavy expense, I would have brought them all with me to Hindustan."

"If they are all as fine as this mare," said the King, "I will purchase every one. Let them be brought."

"If Your Majesty will but have a thousand pieces of gold given to me for the journey, I will return with the whole herd in twenty days."

"Let it be done," said Akbar to Todar Mal, his treasurer.

When Birbal heard about the horse trader, he hurried to speak with the King.

"*Huzur*, you gave him the price of a hundred horses after seeing only one?"

"Well, just a down payment till he brings the herd. But if you had seen this mare, Birbal—they will be cheap at his price."

153

"But has no one at court vouched for this man?"

"Come now, Birbal, suspicion is not a quality for kings. Anyway," said Akbar, changing the subject, "when will the roster of fools be complete?"

"As soon as I add one name," replied Birbal.

The next morning Birbal presented a magnificent scroll to the King—who was shocked, when he opened it, to see the name of Jalaludin Mohammed Akbar Padshah Ghazi, Emperor of Hindustan, heading the list.

"How dare you, Birbal?" shouted Akbar. "What is my name doing on this roll?"

"May I be your sacrifice, O Defender of the Frontiers. But have you not just given an unknown person a fortune in gold? What is that but foolishness?"

"I told you, Birbal," hissed the King through his teeth. "That man is due back here in twenty days . . ."

"Well, if he *does* come," said Birbal smiling, "we will take your name from the top of that list—and put *his* name there in its place!"

Akbar's anger melted—in fact, he could not help laughing. He canceled his plans for a tax on fools as uncollectible—for who can count the cost of folly except for the truly wise?

THE MISER AND THE POET

There was in the city of Fatehpur Sikri a seller of rare perfumes and spices, who, through his clever trading, had become immensely rich. He was, however, a stingy man.

Hearing that in Akbar's capital a poet could attain wealth and fame, a Persian bard made his way to Hindustan and, by bad luck, first presented himself at the mansion of this miser.

The miser invited him in and, nibbling on a crust of dried cheese, listened with pleasure as the minstrel sang the merchant's praises in verse. But when his songs were sung, rather than rewarding the poet from his purse, as was the custom, the miser rose from his table and said:

"Come back tomorrow. I will pay you then."

The poet was a little disappointed, but he suppressed his pangs of hunger with hope of the bountiful reward.

The next morning, as porters began stirring in the bazaar, the Persian made his way back to the miser's house, only to find him going out for the day. The merchant tried to scamper off, but the poet caught him by the sleeve.

"Please, *Huzur*," he cried. "I have come back, as you told me, to collect my reward."

"Reward?" snarled the miser. "Who said anything about a reward?"

The poet was stunned.

"Sir, I would not have stayed so long reciting my songs to you, if you had not given me to understand . . ."

"I gave you to understand that your doggerel is not worth any money, but you were too dense to take a hint."

"But, sir, you gave your word!"

"Exactly," said the miser. "I gave my word, and you can have it. Surely you don't expect me to keep my word once I've given it away?"

"But why did you tell me to come back today? Why did you bother *promising* to pay me?"

"Oh, just to please you. After all, you said kind things that you did not mean—just to please me—so I repaid you the same way. No doubt when you were thinking about your reward last night, you *were* pleased—so there." And cackling at his own wit, the miser scuttled away.

Alone in the street, the Persian raised his fists to heaven and cried:

"If this is how poets are treated in Hindustan, all the stories of the Mughal Kingdom are lies!"

As luck would have it, these words reached the ears of Birbal, who was passing by. When he heard the poet's story, Birbal invited him to a dinner party at his house that night.

"Another prank, no doubt," muttered the poet.

But, laughing, Birbal gave the man a silver coin to stop the hole in his belly. Then he made the poet promise to come.

That night the poet arrived and was treated, along with a dozen other people, to a magnificent feast. But the Persian was astonished to see that as soon as everyone had eaten their fill, the servants rapidly swept up every crumb and set the table again, as if a second dinner was coming.

"This is an odd country," thought the poet. But he said nothing.

At that moment the miser was announced and given the seat of honor. Birbal welcomed him with flattering words and then regaled all the guests with palace gossip.

Meanwhile, the miser began to feel rather hungry. As the banter dragged on and on, he thought: "How is it none of them is thinking of dinner?" Birbal had just finished one long tale and was about to embark upon another, when the miser could suppress the growlings of his stomach no longer. Losing both patience and manners, he thundered:

"Look here, isn't anybody going to bring the food?"

Everyone turned to him, completely amazed.

"Food?" asked Birbal innocently. "But we all had dinner hours ago."

With his jaw dropping, the miser looked incredulously—from the perfect place settings around the table to the satisfied expressions of the guests. Grasping the enormity of this insult, he sprung sputtering to his feet:

"How dare you make a fool of me in this manner? Do you think I am nobody? I am a wealthy merchant in this city! I'll—I'll . . ." And then he collapsed on a silken cushion, in hot tears of shame. "But why?" choked the miser. "Why did you even bother to invite me?"

"Just to please you," replied Birbal with wide-open eyes.

As it dawned on the miser what Birbal meant, he noticed the poet, whom, in his self-importance, he had completely overlooked. He jumped to his feet, furious again.

"Who are you to teach me how to behave?" he shouted. And he bolted for the door.

But as soon as he had turned his back on the company, his blood froze at the sickening whisper of steel.

Slowly coming around, he was horrified to see every guest standing, with all their daggers drawn.

Gulping, he fumbled with the snug knot on his moneybag.

"Oh, all right," he quavered. "Take your stupid reward, poet—not that you deserve it!"

Unable to loose the twisted purse strings, the miser, in frustration, threw his entire pouch of gold at the poet's feet. Then he ran for his life.

Birbal smiled thinly as he turned to the gawking Persian:

"We may sometimes make a show of it, stranger, but you will find we do reward our poets in Hindustan very well."

THE OBEDIENT HUSBAND

One day Birbal was thinking aloud to Akbar:
"Whenever we have to make an important decision, such as drafting laws or going to war, we gather a council of the wisest men in the kingdom and hear their advice."

"That is an intelligent and time-honored custom," said the King.

"And yet," mused Birbal, "it is strange that we do not rather ask their wives."

"Their wives?" said Akbar. "Whatever for?"

"Well," said Birbal. "Have you never noticed how many men follow their wives' orders in everything they do?"

"I don't take orders from women," said Akbar, loftily.

"Ah, but *Huzur*," smiled Birbal. "Are you forgetting the time the ladies of the harem convinced you to dismiss your prime minister, Bairam Khan?"

"Oh, well," mumbled the Emperor. "Possibly in that particular case, if you really want to count it . . . although I was a mere boy. But, Birbal, I can hardly believe all men submit meekly to the orders of their wives!"

"That is the nature of marriage, *Jahanpanah*."

"Would a man obey his wife to defy an Imperial Command?"

"Shall we put it to the test?" asked Birbal.

"Why not?" grinned the King.

So Birbal assembled all the married courtiers and announced:

"Shah Akbar wishes to know how many in this august gathering obey their wives' commands and how many of you command your wives. On your honor—and on pain of death—those who do what their wives tell them are ordered by the King to step ten paces to the left."

There was a tremendous scuffle. When the dust settled, only one young man was seen standing in his original spot—all the others were huddled meekly together against the left wall.

"Ah," beamed the Emperor. "Here is at least one brave fellow who does not let his wife push him around. I shall reward his courage."

"One moment, *Huzur*," said Birbal. "First let me ask him a question. After all, he could be deaf . . ."

"You have no faith in human nature," laughed Akbar.

"On the contrary," said Birbal, "I have too much."

When the young man came forward, Birbal asked why he had stayed put.

"Well, sir, since my pocket was picked a month ago, my wife has told me every day to avoid crowds. So, when everyone else went left, remembering my wife's instructions, I stayed here to the right."

The entire assembly roared with laughter, and the Emperor gave the man a purse of silver saying:

"I must confess that human nature can be even stronger than obedience to the Throne. But," he added, laying a finger of warning aside his nose, "let no one breathe a word of this experiment to the *Queen* . . ."

THE HUNT

A kbar loved to hunt. He was a crack shot with a musket, a superb horseman, and his personal courage—whether on the battlefield or facing an angry tiger—was admired far and wide.

One fine day in April, on the banks of the whispering River Jhelum, the Emperor commanded his nobles to arrange a stupendous hunting party.

"Let the stout-hearted sportsman of Hindustan ride over mountains and meadows in greater hordes than the armies of a dozen lesser kings!" ordered the Great Mughal.

After ten days' preparation, hundreds of beaters surrounded some fifty miles of chosen jungle, driving birds and beasts into a vast trap for the slaughter.

Leaping on a superb black stallion, Akbar called Wazir Birbal to his side.

"Ride with me, my friend. This will be a splendid day!"

And the two galloped off in the forefront of the marksmen, bowmen, lancers, elephants, cheetahs, falconers, skinners, and cooks which made up the royal hunting party. They thundered far into the vast area of forest, which quivered in fear of man.

The Emperor and Birbal out-distanced all the others. At midmorning they paused to rest under a spreading *peepul*[37] tree beside a murmuring brook. Akbar bounded from his horse and splashed water on his face.

At that moment, the hooting of two owls high in the *peepul* tree caught the Emperor's ear. Laughing, he turned to Birbal, who was easing painfully out of his saddle after the hard ride.

"Birbal—surely a man of your learning knows the language of the birds. Tell me what those owls are saying."

Birbal listened thoughtfully and replied:

"*Jahanpanah*, those owls are the heads of two families. One wants his daughter to marry the other's son."

The Emperor was curious.

"Does the son's father agree?"

Birbal listened to the gentle hooting a moment and said:

"He agrees if the girl's father will give him ten empty jungles as a dowry."

Akbar smiled.

"That's a lot of territory. How will the girl's father manage?"

"Just a minute, *Huzur*," continued Birbal, listening. "Ah—he says that if the boy's father will wait two months, he will give him forty empty jungles and more."

"Ask him how he is going to do that, Birbal."

"Yes, he is just saying that the King is so fond of killing animals, the owls will soon have every jungle in India to themselves."

Akbar's gaze fell suddenly to the ground. For a long time he remained silent. Then he mounted his horse and rode back. Birbal followed. When he reached the loudly advancing ranks of hunters, he held up his hand with all the majesty of a man born to command and cried:

"Break the hunt! Set all the animals free! Not the feather of a finch is to be touched!"

From that day until his death Shah Akbar ate meat only three months a year, renounced hunting, and ordered the freedom of all caged birds.

And beneath the owl's *peepul* tree, by the banks of the murmuring brook, he laid out a beautiful garden and raised a marble pavilion, to commemorate the hallowed spot where Jalaludin Mohammed Akbar Padshah Ghazi, Emperor of India, heard from his speechless subjects their just call for mercy.

VOLUME 3

A Companion to the King:
Still More Birbal Tales from the Oral Tradition of India

THE CARAVAN OF FOOLS

One evening in the House of Worship, Akbar sat in the company of learned men, discussing matters of science and philosophy late into the night.

At last Akbar remarked, "The counsel of wise men strengthens our Empire, but foolish people are a curse. We have searched far and wide to fill our Court with sages. Why should we not banish all the fools as well? That way, our society would be perfect."

"A noble plan," said one of the wise men.

"Your kingdom would be heaven on earth," said another.

But Birbal only smiled.

"You do not agree?" asked Akbar.

"O Refuge of the World," said Birbal respectfully. "Shadows make the light lovely by their contrast. So foolishness makes us cherish wisdom. We often learn more from fools than from the wise."

"If that is so," said a jealous courtier, "let Birbal instruct us all. Have him bring the greatest fools in the kingdom to this court."

Akbar smiled.

"What a curious idea! So you shall, Birbal! We have Nine Jewels for wise men at my court. Therefore you shall bring to me, one week from tonight, the *ten* greatest fools in my kingdom."

"Your wish," said Birbal, "is my command."

And he set about the busy, winding streets of Fatehpur Sikri, pausing in the most popular food stalls to watch people go by. He smiled to think how the colors and bustle of the capital had astonished him as a young man, so many years ago.

Near the city gates he saw a man lying on his back in a great mud puddle. The man held his arms stiffly in front of him, while kicking his legs furiously in the air.

"He must be sick," thought Birbal. "I'll help him."

But when Birbal bent over him, the man on the ground shouted:

"Don't touch my hands! Don't touch my hands!"

Birbal jumped back.

"Why? Are you a leper?" he asked.

"Idiot! Anyone can see I am trying to get out of this pot-hole, which I have had the bad luck to fall into!"

"Well, why don't you just get up?"

"Because I would have to use my hands to get up, and any moron can see that if I used my hands, I'd have to move my arms."

"So why can't you move your arms?" asked Birbal.

"I am trying to be patient with you," said the man through his teeth. "I was on my way to buy a length of cloth for my wife. The space between my hands is just the amount she needs. If I change the position of my hands, I'll lose the measurement of her cloth and have to go home empty-handed."

Birbal laughed.

"In that case, let me help you up. But first you must promise to come with me to meet the King."

"The King!" shouted the man in irritation. "Why would I want to meet the King?"

"He will reward you for the visit, and with the reward you can purchase all the cloth your wife needs."

"Oh, well, then . . ."

And the man followed Birbal, still trying to keep his hands carefully spaced.

Shortly after they came across a man riding an old donkey. But the man had a load of firewood piled on top of his head.

"Hey!" shouted the first fool. "Why don't you put the firewood on the donkey's back?"

"Although I would not normally waste my time talking to such an ignorant yokel," sneered the old man, "since I see you are in the company of a refined gentlemen, you may as well know that this donkey is very old. If he has to carry *my* weight, the least *I* can do is take the weight of this firewood upon *myself.*"

Birbal smiled and persuaded the woodcutter to accompany him to Court.

After a while, a man dashed up and collided with Birbal. Both went sprawling in the dust.

"Oaf!" cried the stranger. "Do you think you own the whole road? Didn't you hear me coming?"

"What's your big hurry?" asked Birbal faintly, brushing himself off.

"I am the caller of prayer from that mosque," said the man, pointing to a nearby minaret. "In order to see how far I could be heard, I was trying to catch the sound of my own voice. And I would have made it, too, if you hadn't got in my way."

Laughing, Birbal persuaded him to join his group, and a little farther on, he noticed a fellow on all fours, intently studying the ground.

"Are you a geologist?" asked Birbal.

"A geologist!" snapped the man with contempt. "Certainly not. I am looking for my ring."

"Where did you lose it?" asked Birbal.

"Now, if I *knew* where I lost it, it wouldn't be lost, would it?"

"True," smiled Birbal. "But I meant we might help you find it."

"Well, in that case, I can tell you that I dropped it in my warehouse there, across the street."

"Then you should be looking for it there, not here!" said Birbal.

"That warehouse," said the man patiently, "is as dark as night. I'd never find a ring in *there*. Out here, at least, I can see what I'm doing!"

"Oh, Prince of Thinkers, you *must* come with us," grinned Birbal.

Next the group encountered two men fighting. When Birbal pulled them apart, the first shouted:

"He has set his tiger on my buffalo!"

"Tiger? Buffalo?" asked Birbal. "Where?"

"Well, of course you don't *see* them, you fool! It is just that he overheard me *praying* for a buffalo, and—"

"And I told him that if God would send the likes of *him* a buffalo, *I* would pray for a tiger to go and eat it up!"

"Dog and son of a dog!" barked the first man, lunging at the second.

"Let us take this before the King," said Birbal, ordering the two enemies apart. The men snorted their agreement, each sure that Akbar would see the justice of his cause.

Heading toward the palace, Birbal noticed a beggar creeping on all fours over a patch of sand and weeping.

"What on earth are you doing?" asked Birbal.

"I am bewailing my bad luck, sir. I hid my begging bowl full of copper *paisas* beneath this sand, and now I cannot find it."

"Did you mark the spot?" asked Birbal.

"Well, of course I marked the spot," snapped the beggar. "There was a cloud straight over my hiding place. But now some brigand has taken both cloud and coppers."

"How sad," murmured the members of Birbal's little group.

"Won't you join us?" laughed Birbal.

And finally all eight of these men found themselves in the Sublime Presence of the Mughal King.

"Peacock of the Age," announced Birbal. "I am happy to present you with the ten most foolish men in Fatehpur Sikri." And he described the circumstances under which he had found every one.

Akbar was delighted, and, laughing to the point of tears, he gave splendid rewards to each of the fools before sending them along their way.

But when they had gone, he suddenly remembered Birbal had said the *ten* most foolish men in Fatehpur Sikri.

"There were only *eight*," Akbar objected.

Birbal smiled.

"I think not, *Jahanpanah*. I was counting the King who would set such a task, and the Wazir who would spend a whole day wandering the streets of the city to fulfill it!"

WHO'S LUCK?

There was a silversmith in Fatehpur Sikri, whose metalworking skill was famous to the ends of the Empire. But he was famous for another thing, too. Everybody said that one look at his ugly face would bring bad luck all day.

Akbar felt sorry for this man's reputation, and decided to improve his fortunes by inviting him to Court. He sent Birbal to fetch him.

But, no sooner had the silversmith bowed before the Peacock Throne than a messenger dashed in, announcing that the Province of Bengal was in revolt. Hurriedly, Akbar called a council of his generals and dispatched Man Singh with an army of picked men to crush the rebels.

Confident that General Man Singh would restore peace, he returned to the Hall of Public Audience only to meet the court physician, who confided that the Queen had fallen seriously ill. Akbar rushed to the Queen's residence. In fact, Jodh Bai was only jealous of a beautiful Kashmiri princess who had come to serve in the palace. Akbar had to go to a great deal of trouble to bring a smile back to her lips.

Tired, exasperated and hungry, the Emperor returned to the *Diwan* and shouted for the Head Chef to serve his lunch. But the terrified cook stammered that he had believed Akbar had gone off with the expedition to Bengal, and so he had sent the King's lunch after the soldiers!

"Bring me anything, so long as I can eat it!" thundered Akbar. And, as he settled moodily upon the Peacock Throne, he noticed the trembling silversmith, still waiting patiently upon the Imperial pleasure.

"This man really does bring bad luck," thought Akbar. "My kingdom, my home life, even the royal kitchens started to fall apart as soon as I laid eyes upon him. What people say is true. Such a man is a threat to all around him. It is unsafe to let him wander free in this world."

And, clapping his hands, Akbar ordered the unfortunate silversmith to be thrown in the darkest dungeon.

But Birbal, who was standing quietly by the throne, stepped forward and said:

"*Huzur* . . ."

"*Now* what?" shouted the King. "Don't tell me the astrologers have predicted an earthquake!"

"No," smiled Birbal. "But this man should hardly go to jail."

"Shouldn't he?," said the King. "My dear Birbal, his very face is a plague!"

"You are looking at the thing wrong way about, O Full Moon. This poor silversmith woke up today with no plans but to tinker away in his little shop. Now you have brought him here and, just for paying homage the King, he has lost his freedom! If *his* face has been unlucky for *you, Jahanpanah*, stop to think how unlucky *your* face has been for *him!*"

Akbar rubbed his jowls, where slowly a smile began to spread. Finally, laughing out loud, he rewarded the smith with a hundred ounces of virgin silver and sent him on his fretful way.

THE WITNESS OF
A MANGO TREE

One of Akbar's courtiers, named Vikram, was exceedingly dishonest. He used his position to take great sums of money from the poor. But he always concealed his evil nature from the King.

One day Vikram was reclining under a mango tree, when a very old man, who worked on his estate, approached him and said:

"Master, my elder brother has fallen ill in the next village, and I must make the journey to visit him and look after his wife and sons. But I cannot leave my life's savings in my hut—it would be unsafe. So please allow me to entrust this bag of silver *paisa* with you."

"How many are there?" said Vikram in a bored way.

"One thousand five hundred," quavered the old man.

Now Vikram sat up. How on earth had this old man come to save so much silver? "Probably pilfering it from me," he thought. But aloud he said:

"Hand it here. It will be waiting for you on your return."

But when the old man's brother recovered and he made the tiring journey home, Vikram refused to see him. The chief servant at Vikram's mansion said:

"The master says you never gave him anything, and he is outraged that you should make any such claim. Begone, before I have you whipped as well as thrown out."

Weak with fear and distress, the old man staggered off the estate. Not knowing what to do, he turned his weary steps towards the house of Birbal.

When he heard the story, Birbal issued an official summons to Vikram and the old man. Both appeared the following morning before the Emperor himself.

"*Jahanpanah*," said Vikram with a scowl. "I live by your grace and my inherited wealth. I do not need to take a coin from anyone—let alone the savings of a wretched old man. After long years of keeping this lazy servant on my estate, he repays my kindness with this shoddy attempt to steal some of my money."

The King asked the old man to tell his side of the story. When he had finished, Birbal asked:

"When you gave your bag of silver to Lord Vikram, were there any witnesses?"

The old man thought and thought. But then he had to admit, in the face of Vikram's triumphant smile, that the two of them had been entirely alone beneath a mango tree.

But Vikram's smile melted when Birbal shouted:

"A mango tree! Why, you old fool! Why didn't you tell me that before? We shall summon the mango tree as a witness, and *it* can settle the whole affair."

"*Huzur*," protested Vikram. "Wazir Birbal is famous for his jokes, but now he is simply wasting everyone's time."

"Yes, really, Birbal," said the King. "Do you actually think—"

"*Jahanpanah*, I have never wasted your time before. It is only right to summon any witness that can testify."

"But can a mango tree testify?" asked Akbar.

"It can," smiled Birbal.

"As you wish," sighed the King. And Birbal said to the old man:

"You go and tell the mango tree to come. Hurry, for His Majesty is waiting."

Baffled, the old man picked up his staff and hobbled off along the dusty road to Vikram's estate.

"How in the world am I going to bring a mango tree to Court?" he sighed. "But how can I disobey the Emperor?"

While he was gone, Birbal paced back and forth. Impatiently he called out, as if to himself:

"That stupid old man! Why doesn't he hurry?"

He paced some more and then exclaimed:

"Doesn't he realize we could have solved this thing by now, if only he had come back?"

Again he fretfully walked up and down.

"I regret I ever listened to that lazy old fool!" cried Birbal, biting his finger in fury. "How far away can that blasted mango tree be?"

Unable to stand it any longer, Vikram interrupted:

"Birbal, have patience. By now he's only had time to *reach* the mango tree, let alone *return*."

"Humph!" grumbled Birbal, and continued pacing to and fro. But at this precise moment, he took note of the sundial in the garden.

When the old man at last returned, he trembled as he prostrated himself before the Peacock Throne:

"I gave your Imperial Order to the mango tree, *Huzur*, but it said not a word, nor would it come."

"Never mind," drawled Birbal. "That mango tree has already testified, here in this court."

The old man's jaw dropped. Vikram goggled at Birbal.

"What are you talking about?" asked Akbar.

"May your shadow never grow less, O Star of the Age," said Birbal. "Lord Vikram not only knew which mango tree the old man had in mind, but he told us precisely how long this old man would take to reach it and return. His prediction was fulfilled with such exactness, I can only conclude that Vikram and the old man did in fact meet under that very mango tree, and this old man's story is the truth."

The courtiers murmured in astonishment.

"Then you lied to me!" shouted Akbar, shoving a finger in Vikram's face. Vikram was so shaken, he stammered a terrified confession.

"Anyone who would lie to me is a threat," thundered Akbar. "And anyone who steals from my subjects is my enemy."

He ordered Vikram to pay his old servant double the sum he had stolen and exiled him forever from the Mughal Court.

THE TEST

Mullah Babrak was a hair-splitting theologian, whom Akbar had appointed to some petty post.

One day the Mullah asked the Emperor, "How can Your Majesty exalt this village Hindu, Birbal, over some of the greatest nobles of Islam?"

Then he said something that had long gnawed at Akbar's heart.

"No wonder it is Sultan Suleiman of Istanbul, and not you, whom men call Commander of the Faithful."

Akbar frowned. "I do not have Birbal at my side just because he is a Hindu. His advice is more valuable to me than fame."

"But, *Jahanpanah*, you have a court full of wise men who can give you advice. I myself can give you advice."

"Yes," said Akbar, "but I have yet to see the problem that Birbal cannot solve."

Mullah Babrak lost no time. "If I can pose such a problem, will you appoint me in his place?"

Akbar surveyed the rat-like glitter in Mullah Babrak's eye, but after a moment's reflection, he agreed.

On the day of the contest, the Court was packed, for Babrak was known as a tiger of debate. Noblemen prayed for Birbal's fall, while harem beauties anxiously nibbled *halwa* from behind a hidden screen.

Babrak strode before the Peacock Throne with the pride of Pharaoh.

"I shall ask two questions, Birbal, and if you are unable to answer either, you shall lose your place and possessions to me."

Birbal nodded.

"The first question is," boomed Babrak, "How many stars adorn the Heavens?"

"Through a special process of divination," answered Birbal at once, "I have learned that the number of stars in the sky is exactly the same as the number of hairs in your beard. If you will allow me to pluck them out one by one, we shall presently know the tally."

Laughter rippled through the Court, but Mullah Babrak was outraged—was his beard not the symbol of his reverend learning? Still, without answering, he let his second question fly:

"Impudent though you are, I shall give you one more chance: Where, precisely, is the center of the earth?"

"You are standing on it—precisely," replied Birbal.

"How can you prove that?" sneered Babrak.

"I do not need to prove it, because I know it," said Birbal. "However, if you would like to prove it to yourself, simply pace west from here, counting your steps, until you reach the world's end. Then return to this spot and repeat the process to the north, south, and east. You will discover in every case that the distance works out exactly the same."

Turning with exasperation to the Emperor, Babrak implored:

"This man is a mere trickster, *Huzur*, winning points through useless wit. How can we accept such answers to serious metaphysical questions?"

"I might agree with you entirely," smiled Akbar, "if *you* would agree to put them to the test . . ."

But Mullah Babrak preferred to preserve his beard and, with many other courtiers who had been stung before him, nursed his jealousy in silence.

CHECKMATE

P rince Salim grew to love the pleasures of life more than his duties. He fell in with some of the shadier noblemen at Akbar's Court and even began to listen to their doubts about Wazir Birbal.

One day as the Emperor and his son were inspecting the royal stables, Salim said:

"Father, you are considered a clever man. Why do you need to keep this so-called sage, Birbal, hovering at your elbow?"

"It is well that you should ask," said Akbar, "but it is better that Birbal himself should answer."

And though the Prince blushed when he heard his question repeated to Birbal, Birbal himself merely told a story:

"Once upon a time, O Prince of Bright Promise, there was a King in ancient India with many wives and many steeds and many jesters and vast, whispering gardens—and yet he was bored with life.

"So the King promised a great reward to anyone who could invent a truly original pastime. After many months, an ancient wise man approached the throne and presented a rosewood checkerboard and many tiny figurines—for he had invented the game of chess.[38]

"When the wise man explained the complex strategies of chess, the King was overjoyed and offered him any reward—up to half his kingdom.

"But the old man bowed his gray head and murmured:

"'I am a scholar with most of my life behind me, *Maharaj*. What use are material blessings to me? I only ask for a little rice. Just put one grain of rice on the first square of the chessboard, then double that number of grains on the second square, then double that amount on the third square, and keep going, until you have put rice on all sixty-four squares of the board.'

"The King exchanged smiles with his courtiers at the dotard's simplicity, and he commanded some rice to be brought.

"On the first square he put one grain of rice, looked up at the old wise man and smiled. The scholar remained as impassive as a statue.

"On the second square, the King put two grains of rice, and smiled at the wise man again.

"On the third square, the King put four grains of rice; on the fourth, eight grains. On the fifth, he put sixteen grains of rice. On the sixth, he put 32 grains. On the seventh square, he put 64 grains, and 128 on the eighth. On the ninth square, he *would* have put 256 grains of rice . . . but there was no more room.

"The king looked up at the old wise man, and a shadow of concern passed across the royal brow. For the first time the old wise man smiled. And it was the smile of a lynx.

"The king nervously called his Treasurer, who calculated the rice needed for the tenth square.

"'512 grains, Sire,' said the Treasurer.

"On the eleventh square, 1,024 grains were needed, and 2,048 on the twelfth.

"By the twentieth square, over a half a million grains of rice were required. The Treasurer, who was calculating ahead, looked at the King in alarm.

"By the twenty-fifth square, the amount of rice had soared to nearly seventeen million grains, and by the thirty-second square—which was only half-way across the board—over two billion grains were needed.

"In the end, there was not enough rice or wealth in the kingdom to meet the old scholar's demand—and so he, instead, became King."

Salim was silent, but Akbar turned to his son and said:

"Either a king takes counsel of the wise, or the wise make folly of the king."

"Just so, *Jahanpanah*," smiled Birbal.

And although Prince Salim nodded, he was jealous of this man who seemed to know his father's heart more intimately than he did his own.

THE COURAGEOUS CHEAT

There was once a miser, of whom people said:
"He will part with his life, but not with a cowry shell!"
Year by year the miser had hoarded splendid jewelry, worth thousands of gold *mohurs*. This he kept in a beautiful rosewood box. Every night he would open the box and caress his jewels, gloating and gazing till his eyes were sore.

But one day the miser's house caught fire. As smoke billowed from the hissing timbers, his servants raced into the street, shouting: "Save your lives!"

The miser dueled with the flames, struggling to reach his rosewood box. But he was beaten back by the intolerable heat, and his servants dragged him gasping from the fire.

"My box!" he croaked. "I will reward anyone who will bring out my rosewood box!"

Among the crowd which had gathered to watch the satisfying sight of a miser's house on fire was a young man who was addicted to wine, but who seldom had a copper to his name. "This is the chance of a lifetime," he thought.

"I will fetch your treasure chest," said the young man, "on one condition."

"Name it," grunted the miser, wiping soot from his eyes.

"If I save the box, I will give you from it only whatever I like. Do you agree?"

The miser wrestled with his instincts. "After all," he thought, "let him take a gem or two, so long as he returns the others to me." Then part of the roof fell, giving rise to a fountain of fire, and the miser hastily agreed.

Caring nothing for his life, the young man dodged through the snarling flames, found the box and returned, singed but triumphant, to the arms of a cheering crowd. The miser, in his cackling way, cheered him loudest of all.

But his grin froze in horror as he watched the rescuer open the box, scoop out *all* the jewels, and hand it back empty to its owner.

"I have risked my life, and you have agreed to let me give you whatever I *like*. Well, the box is what I'd *like* to give you."

The miser howled to the skies, and even his neighbors, who had never liked him, protested on his behalf.

"Even we who were just standing by," said the baker, "thought you would reward yourself with only *part* of the treasure."

"Didn't you hear him agree? And haven't I done *just* what I said?"

"I admit that," said the spice merchant, "but you are twisting common sense."

"Oh, no," laughed the young man, "I think I've done the most sensible thing in my life!"

"Thievery," sobbed the old man. "Plain thievery!"

"It is a matter for Birbal," said the tent maker.

"Why bring him into it?" objected the young man.

But the crowd shouted: "Yes! To Birbal!" And they hustled him and the sooty miser off.

When Wazir Birbal had heard the case, he rubbed his beard and frowned. Then he said:

"The letter of the law must be upheld. It may sometimes run counter to the truth in men's hearts, but when we make a contract, we must not stray from it so much as a comma. The deal between these two should stand."

"This is injustice . . ." the miser groaned.

"Silence!" commanded Birbal. "A man must stick to his word." Then, turning to the young man, he asked: "Do you see it my way?"

"As if we could see through the same eye, *Huzur*," the young man grinned.

"Good," said Birbal. "Now, just for the education of these good people, let us review your agreement and show them how the law applies. You opened the box and you liked the gems."

"Who wouldn't?" said the young man.

"Of course," smiled Birbal. "And what did you think of the box?"

"It is well made, but I don't much care if I never see it again."

"Fine," remarked Birbal. "I hope you people are paying close attention. Now please repeat exactly the conditions this despicable miser agreed to."

"Well," said the young man, tossing his head in triumph, "he said that if I saved the box he would let me give him from it whatever I liked."

"Splendid, splendid," chuckled Birbal, rubbing his hands. "Now give him the gems."

The miser gawked suddenly at the face of the Wazir—which had grown stern as granite.

"What?" choked the young man.

"Give him the gems. You promised to give him whatever *you* liked. Well, you have just told me you *liked* the gems, and you did *not* like the box. So the gems are rightfully *his*, and the box is rightfully *yours*. You have agreed to keep your word."

"Sir," shrieked the youth, "you are twisting my words—this is sheer injustice!"

"If the miser had known you were going to hand him an empty box, he would not have made any agreement with you at all. You twisted your own words."

The young man hung his head in bitterness. After gnawing his lip thoughtfully for a moment, he said:

"Sir, I am prepared to share the gems with this man."

But Birbal scowled. "You heard my feelings about the letter of the law."

"But please, sir, then let me keep just one jewel for risking my life like a hero."

"Like a hero?" said Birbal, raising an eyebrow. "When a man puts his life in danger to climb through another man's window at night, we do not call him a hero. But I will let the miser decide the matter of one gem."

And turning to the miser he said: "Old man, your face may be blackened by soot, but your heart is blackened with greed. Stinginess nearly caught you in its web today. Are you ready to change?"

The miser thought a moment. Then, bowing to the Wazir, he said:

"*Huzur*, no gem in that box is worth less than a hundred *mohurs*. Let the brave lad choose whichever suits him best, and may he prosper."

AKBAR DECIDES
TO BECOME A HINDU

One morning, after the tongues of debate had echoed far into the night at Akbar's Assembly of the Wise, the King turned to Birbal and said:

"My family have been Muslims for generations, but I myself am married to a Rajput Princess and the majority of my people are Hindus. I do not see any difference between the *inner* meaning of Hinduism and Islam. Would it not give greater confidence to my subjects if I became a Brahmin like you?"

Birbal smiled. "*Huzur*, you are a good man. Surely that is enough."

"Birbal, you say this from respect for the faith of my ancestors, but my mind is made up. I shall travel to Varanasi and be baptized in the holy river Ganges. Arrange for the appropriate ceremony."

Birbal bowed in obedience and the very next day a great entourage set out from the dry hills of Northern India into the wide, emerald valley of the Ganges.

One the evening along the way, when the bird chorus was subsiding into sleepy murmurs, Birbal invited his sovereign to stroll along the banks of the swirling river. There they encountered two peasants knee-deep in a pool, scrubbing a pair of miserable donkeys with all their might. Akbar called out:

"Are you trying to skin those poor beasts on their feet? What need is there to scrape so hard?"

"Sir," replied the first peasant, "we are trying to turn these donkeys into horses."

"Into horses?" snorted Akbar.

"Truly, sir," said the second peasant. "A wise man told us that if we scrubbed these donkeys hard enough—and if we made the right offerings to the gods—we should have two horses in an hour's time!"

"That," drawled Akbar, "is the stupidest thing I have heard in my life."

"Oh?" bristled the first peasant. "Then you have perhaps not heard of our Muslim King, who proposes to become a Hindu merely by dipping in the Ganges."

Akbar cast a suspicious glance at Birbal, who, however, was gazing with innocence at the golden splinters of sunset upon the river.

"Was the wise man who told you these things Wazir Birbal?" asked the King.

"Yes, sir," smiled the peasants.

"Then perhaps we should return to Sikri, Birbal," said Akbar. "For I see that a man must change from the heart, not through outward rites."

"Mysterious," murmured Birbal with the thin hint of a smile, "are the ways of God . . ."

THE LOAN

There were two grain merchants in Fatehpur Sikri who were great friends. Dinesh, however, was an honest man, while Anand, unknown to his friend, was a thief.

One day Anand visited the shop of Dinesh and pretended, with many sighs, to be very unhappy.

"I have fallen on hard times," he confessed to his friend. "And if I cannot scrape together five hundred gold *mohurs*, I shall be ruined."

"What!" cried Dinesh. "Do you insult my friendship by not asking me for this trifle?"

He took five hundred *mohurs* of flashing gold from his money chest and poured them out before Anand.

"Thank you, brother," wept Anand. "May your shadow never grow less."

Many months passed, and the two friends often met. Dinesh noticed that Anand seemed ever more prosperous, and he began to wonder about his loan. But he was too honorable ever to ask, for he remembered the Arabian proverb:

> *"He who loans money should never mention it,*
> *and he who borrows should never forget."*

Then one day a caravan in which Dinesh had heavily invested was attacked by Baluchi[39] raiders in the desert. Dinesh stood to lose everything he owned. For many days he hesitated, but at last he went to the house of his friend, Anand. A slave dressed in the finest silk answered the door.

"What do you want?" scowled the slave.

"Tell your master that his good friend Dinesh is here. Tell him that I would never have spoken of our loan, but I am desperate, and I need the five hundred gold *mohurs* I gave him long ago."

Leaving him in the street, the slave disappeared. When he returned, he shouted:

"My master knows nobody by the name you mention, and he certainly will not give you five hundred pieces of gold. He is a rich merchant and has borrowed nothing from anyone."

The slave slammed the door in Dinesh's face.

Amazed at his friend's dishonesty and sick with fear, Dinesh staggered home. When his wife heard the story, she decided she must seek help. Veiling herself, she went to visit her friend, who happened to be the cook at the house of Birbal. The cook had often spoken of her master's wit and influence at Court.

When Birbal heard of Dinesh's problem, he told the cook:

"We shall send a barrel of grain to both Dinesh and Anand. We will tell them that His Majesty would like to sell a thousand such barrels from the royal storehouses, but first he wishes to see how much a single barrel will fetch. Each merchant will sell his barrel in the open market. Then have them bring the proceeds of their sales to me."

Into each barrel of grain, however, Birbal secretly dropped one gold coin.

When Dinesh received his consignment, he thought: "A thousand barrels! What a stroke of luck. If the King chooses me to act as his broker, I can rebuild my fortunes. Let me go find a buyer right away."

But when he inspected the contents of the barrel, he found the gold coin.

"Lucky I opened it before it sold," he thought.

At the same time, Anand received his barrel and discovered his gold coin.

"What luck!" he cried. "Akbar has millions of these—the Treasury will never miss one." He gave it to his little son, telling him to place it in the money box in his shop. And when the cook at Anand's house met with Birbal's cook in the bazaar, the tale was told.

When the two merchants had completed their sales, they went to Wazir Birbal.

Dinesh gave Birbal a fair price for the barrel of grain. He also handed him the gold *mohur*, saying:

"I am sure the Royal Treasurer will be relieved when he finds out where this coin was misplaced."

Birbal thanked Dinesh for his honesty.

When Anand came before the Wazir, he claimed to have sold his barrel for a much higher price than Dinesh—because he wanted to get the King's business. He gave Birbal the price of the barrel of grain and added the value of the gold coin, of which he said nothing.

Then Birbal summoned both merchants together. Dinesh could hardly look his former friend in the face. Anand pretended not to know the man he had robbed.

"Why have you failed to return the gold coin from the barrel of grain, Anand, as your honest friend here did?"

Anand was taken aback.

"Th . . . there was no gold coin in the barrel of grain, Your Excellency . . . there must be some mistake!"

At that moment Anand's son arrived and said:

"I have come, Father."

Beads of sweat burst out upon Anand's forehead.

"Who sent for you?" he demanded angrily.

"*You* did, Father!"

Birbal gazed at the crooked merchant with a half-smile. He had sent for the boy in his father's name.

"Here is the gold coin which you found in the grain barrel," continued the little boy, "just as you ordered me to bring."

"There was no coin the grain barrel!" roared Anand.

"But there *was!*" stammered the lad. "Don't you remember? You said it was good luck. You said . . ."

"Enough!" shouted Anand.

"Yes, enough," murmured Birbal. "A man who is dishonest about one gold coin will easily pilfer five hundred. But I will give you a choice. Either repay your honest friend here double the amount you borrowed from him—"

"Double!" shrieked Anand.

"Or," continued Birbal darkly, "face the wrath of Shah Akbar for the crime of stealing from the Crown."

Anand swallowed in terror.

"I . . . I will pay . . . ." he croaked.

And the fame of Birbal grew.

THE HEART'S DESIRE

There was once a very dull Brahmin in Fatehpur Sikri, whose fondest wish was to earn the reputation of a great scholar, or pundit.

"I would die happy," he confided to Birbal, "if only I could hear myself addressed as *'punditji'⁴⁰* by rich and poor."

"What are you willing to sacrifice for this honor?" asked Birbal.

"Oh, there is nothing I would not do," exclaimed the Brahmin with passion.

"Try study," said Birbal dryly.

"Oh, *well*," protested the Brahmin. "There must be a less tedious method than *that*."

Birbal thought for a moment. "Well, there may be."

Heading for a nearby tavern, Birbal told some drunken local wags about the Brahmin's secret dream.

"What, that imbecile!" laughed one of the sots aloud.

"He can hardly even read his name!" chortled another.

"Oh, we'll call him *'punditji'*, you may be sure," leered a third.

And soon there was hardly a person in the Sikri bazaar who did not guffaw and shout whenever they saw the hapless Brahmin in the streets.

"O Learned One! O Genius of the Age! O Sublime Thinker of Perfumed Thoughts! How have we deserved the blessing of one so profoundly schooled in our unworthy midst?"

It came to the point where even the urchins chased after him, hurling stones and calling: *"Punditji! Pundit-ji!! Oh, P-uu-undit-ji!!!"*

But, strange to tell, it was not long before the Brahmin's annoyance melted away and those jabs became like music to his ears. The fact was he had never wanted more than the *name* of a scholar, and now, thanks to Birbal, his life's ambition had been fulfilled. He remained eternally grateful.

When Akbar asked Birbal to explain the Brahmin's curious behavior, Birbal merely recited this couplet:

> *"Though each be given what his heart desires,*
> *—it may be, in truth, what he least requires."*

Birbal's *Khichdi*

Once in the bitter cold of winter, the Emperor, flanked by his ministers and attendants, was taking a stroll in the Palace garden when Birbal said:

"To gain money men will risk their lives, but to save it they will risk their souls."

"Such a person exists only in Birbal's imagination," said a jealous courtier.

"It is true, *Maharaj*," smiled Birbal, "If this courtier would care to wager the money needed to make the experiment, I can prove my point."

Akbar laughed.

"What do you propose?"

"That a reward of one thousand gold coins be offered to any man who will stand shoulder-deep in yonder lily pond over night."

The King went over to the side of the tank and, kicking off one silken slipper, disturbed its shimmering surface with his toe. Immediately he jerked back.

"The water is ice-cold even now, Birbal! A man who spent a whole night in there would perish."

"That is the challenge," Birbal replied.

"I am ready enough to put up the reward," sniffed the courtier, "for only a madman would try it."

But that evening Birbal brought a young Brahmin to Court.

"I am very poor, *Maharaj*," said the Brahmin to the King. "If I die, my family will not be worse off. But if I survive, this reward will be our fortune."

"Do you accept this candidate?" asked Akbar.

"I do," smiled the courtier, "so long as he uses no source of warmth besides his own skin." He saw the Brahmin was all bones and thought he had no chance of ever seeing the dawn.

So, stripping to his loin cloth, the Brahmin entered the pond, as two Imperial guards stood watch at the water's edge.

When, after what seemed an eternity of frozen pain, the sunrise at last scattered its dancing flames across the pool, the Brahmin called to the guards, who dragged his stiff limbs from the water and carried him chattering to the King.

"Lord of the Horizons," said one of the guards to Akbar, "this fellow has fulfilled his pledge."

"Give him shawls and blankets," cried the Emperor, "and let a hot brazier be brought."

And when the Brahmin's blood had once again begun to flow, Akbar turned to the jealous courtier and said:

"Give this brave soul his due."

"Just a moment," said the nobleman, squinting at the Brahmin and biting his lip. "I have one question for the man. What did you *do* all night as you stood there in the pond?"

"Do?" stuttered the Brahmin. "What *was* there to do? I just *stood* there."

"Did you look at anything?"

"Well, yes," recalled the man. "I let my thoughts wander by watching the palace lights."

"Ah-ha!" grinned the courtier. "Then you derived warmth from those distant lamps! You did not fulfill the conditions. You do not deserve the reward."

"Be fair," chided Akbar.

"Sire, the conditions were: no source of warmth besides his own skin."

And this the King could not deny. But he looked at Birbal, expecting that his friend would have something to say on the matter. Instead, Birbal rose, saying:

"I concede defeat. And in honor of this insightful courtier, let him be the guest of honor at a feast in my house tonight, where Your Majesty's presence is also most humbly requested."

"So be it," said Akbar, shaking his head.

But that night, nearly an hour after the dinner guests had assembled, there was still no sign of food.

"What are we having?" hinted the King to his host.

"*Khichdi*,"[41] said Birbal. "Let me go to the kitchen and see when it will be ready."

Returning after a few minutes, he said: "Not long."

But a full hour passed, and the King's stomach audibly growled.

"Birbal, this *khichdi* is taking some time."

"I will check its progress with the chef," said Birbal politely. And again he returned, saying: "It will be soon."

But after another hour, a mutiny of protest was welling up among the guests. Akbar jumped to his feet and shouted:

"Birbal, you must have the stupidest cook in Hindustan if he can't make a simple *khichdi* in twenty minutes! This time *I* will talk to him, and if it isn't ready, he can prepare to lose his head!"

Storming into the kitchen—with Birbal and all the noblemen at his heels—the King froze to an astonished halt when he saw the cooking fire blazing, but the huge *khichdi* cauldron suspended from the ceiling—eight feet above the flames!

"By my father's beard, Birbal! What idiocy is this?"

"Excuse me, Your Majesty?" said Birbal, blinking dumbly. "What is wrong?"

"What is wrong?" spluttered the famished monarch. "Are you mad?"

"But, Sire, we have flame, food, the pot—what else is needed for cooking?"

"But the *distance* between them!" objected Akbar.

"Ah," smiled Birbal. "But if a freezing man may live simply by *looking* at the distant lights of the palace, why can't the *khichdi* cook from the warmth of fire only a few feet away?"

The Emperor and the noblemen all burst into laughter, while the guest of honor gnashed his teeth. Turning to the jealous courtier, Akbar asked:

"The point is well taken,—now will you pay?"

"I will pay, Your Majesty," seethed the envious noble. "But, for God's sake, now let us eat!"

So, amid great merry-making, the guests returned to the table. Only Akbar lingered in the kitchen, putting his hand on Birbal's sleeve and saying:

"Friend, I see how the Brahmin risked his life to *gain* money—but you said that to *save* money, man would risk even his soul . . ."

"Sire," smiled Birbal. "The greedy nobleman was ready to perjure his honor and cheat the poor—is there any surer way to lose one's soul?"

THE MIND READER

Once a *fakir*[42] came to Fatehpur Sikri and amazed the entire Court with conjuring tricks.

"I am even capable," he told the astonished Court, "of reading people's minds."

There was a gasp of wonder and delight. Immediately he was pressed with a hundred requests to read somebody or other's mind. But when he held up his hand, there was a sudden hush.

"I *could* reveal your thoughts if I wanted to, but that would be impolite. It has rightly been said that if the thoughts of any man, however outwardly pious, were openly seen for as little as ten seconds, there is not a jury in the land which would not sentence him to hang."

The crowd nodded gravely at this sage observation.

But Birbal realized this "miracle worker" was just a fraud, who would soon enrich himself at the expense of many gullible nobles. So he said:

"You know, I am something of a mind reader myself."

"Really?" said the *fakir*, annoyed at this intrusion. "You must tell us about it some time."

"Oh, but I'll do more than that," chirped Birbal. "I'll demonstrate it to you here and now. I will read *your* mind."

Akbar leaned forward from his throne with interest.

"Go on," the King prodded.

"Your Majesty," said Birbal, screwing up his face in fearful concentration, "this man is thinking that his fondest wish is for your prosperity and long life and for new worlds of glory in the reign of your son."

The *fakir* snapped at Birbal: "I had *no* such—"

But he bit his tongue abruptly, as he felt the King's glare upon him.

"As a matter of fact," he gulped, "those *were* my thoughts exactly."

And late upon the road away from Fatehpur Sikri, a good deal of which the *fakir* had put behind him before the moon had risen that night, he paused to advise a second miracle man, who was headed toward the city:

"If you're bound for Sikri, friend, forget it. There is no market for us there."

CARAVANSERAI

One day Birbal and Akbar were returning from a stroll in the Palace garden, when they discovered a holy man, half-naked and with matted hair, snoozing against a royal pavilion.

"*Baba*," said Akbar, prodding the *sadhu* awake. "How did you get in here?"

"How did *you* get here?" asked the mystic, rubbing his eyes.

Akbar and Birbal exchanged glances.

"I live here," said the Emperor. "This is the Palace."

"Palace?" asked the holy man, looking around him in wonder. "I see no Palace. Only a caravanserai."

"Birbal," said the King, struggling to keep his patience. "Please inform this bemused ascetic that this is no flophouse for wanderers."

"Your shoulder, O venerable *fakir*, is resting against the very mansion of Akbar, Pillar of the Age," said Birbal.

But the old man merely turned toward the Emperor:

"Who lived here before you?"

"Before me?" said Akbar. "Why, my father, the Emperor Humayun."

"And before him?"

"Before him it was Sher Shah, the usurper."

"And before him?"

"Well, then it was my grandfather, Babur."

"And you call this place, where people come and spend a few nights and pass along, anything but a caravanserai?"

Birbal and Akbar turned to one another and smiled.

"So is the whole world, *baba*, no more than a cool resting place on a strenuous journey," said Birbal.

"You will enjoy this world," said the *sadhu*, "only if you treat it so."

"Is there anything I can offer you, Father of Insight?" asked the King. "For this lesson you may choose any reward from the riches of my realm."

"Then give me the sun, O Shadow of God Upon the Earth, for at this moment you are standing between me and its warm rays."

Chuckling and moving aside, Akbar and Birbal left the old *sanyasin* in peace.

SLAVE AND MASTER

One fine day at Fatehpur Sikri, a well-known merchant and a stranger came into the Royal Presence. The Emperor knew the merchant.

"Sayyid Hussein," said Akbar, "What brings you to court?"

"As you know, *Huzur*," said the merchant, "I have been a respectable trader at Fatehpur Sikri for seven years. Before I came here, I lived in Kabul. This man was my slave, until he ran away with my valuables. Today I saw him in the bazaar, caught ahold of him, and now I ask Your Majesty to restore my property to me."

"*Jahanpanah*," cried the stranger. "This man is lying through his teeth. His name is not Sayyid Hussein. His name is Murad, and he was *my* slave until he ran away from Kabul with many treasures stolen from my house. After seeking him for seven years, at last I found him here at Fatehpur Sikri."

"Your Majesty," smiled the merchant. "You know me yourself. I can bring witnesses who will testify that this man was my slave. He is a clever liar . . ."

"No, *he* is lying!" shrieked the stranger.

"Silence," thundered the Emperor. "Birbal will decide."

Birbal, who had been listening, stepped up to the men and inspected each of them closely.

"A difficult case," he murmured. "I shall have to find the truth by meditation. I shall close my eyes and pray for wisdom. Meanwhile, both you men lie face down upon the ground."

Mystified, the trader and the stranger followed Wazir Birbal's command. They lay down with their faces buried in the thick, Persian carpets before the throne.

After a long silence, Birbal slowly opened his eyes. "God has revealed the truth," he announced. "Please call the Royal Executioner."

Akbar snapped his fingers, and the executioner ran in, fondling his ax.

"When I point to the guilty man," said Birbal, "you will instantly chop off his head. Do you understand?"

"Yes, Birbal *Sahib*," said the executioner.

"Raise your ax," said Birbal. The executioner lifted it above his head. Akbar leaned forward with interest.

Birbal waited for a long moment and then shouted, "Now!"

With a start, Sayyid Hussein leapt to his feet. His face was red, and sweat poured off his brow.

"Forgive me, Your Majesty," he pleaded, gasping.

The Emperor shook his head. "You are a liar, a runaway, and a thief," he said. "But what do you say, stranger? Have you searched seven years for such an unworthy servant? If he will repay all he has stolen, will you set him free?"

"You are right, *Jahanpanah*," choked the stranger, rubbing his own neck in fear. "Such a servant is not worth having."

"Then," said Akbar, "you shall repay the stranger from Kabul twice what you stole, and then, if your shadow ever again dishonors my Empire, from the Hindu Kush to the shores of Bengal, you will forfeit your miserable head."

And the executioner led him away.

SLEIGHT OF HAND

Once Birbal came across Akbar and Jodh Bai, his beautiful Queen, watching the moon from a marble pavilion. Respectfully, he turned away, but the Emperor cried out:

"Birbal, come and amuse us by telling stories."

"Hearing is obedience, *Huzur.*"

So Birbal spun tales within tales of the heroes of old.

But after a while the King's mind wandered, and he had a mischievous thought. As Birbal continued to narrate the adventures of Rustam, the Persian hero, Akbar stood up, stretched, went to the balcony, watched the silver shavings of the moon dance upon the river, and then came back and sat down—only now he placed himself so that Birbal was *between* him and the Queen.

After a few moments had passed, chuckling inside, Akbar casually leaned back and gave the Queen a hard pinch. Suppressing a yelp, she looked around. The King was studying the moon intently, so she could only conclude it had been Birbal. Indignantly, she smacked him on the cheek.

Without a second's hesitation, Birbal turned and slapped the King.

Astonished, Akbar leapt to his feet, tottering with rage.

"What do you think you are doing?" he shouted.

"Sire, *you* sent a message to the Queen," smiled Birbal. "Well, *Jahanpanah*, the answer has come back."

BANISHMENT

A s Prince Salim grew older, he also grew more wayward, and frequently displeased Akbar. On one occasion, the Emperor was so annoyed with Salim's failure in a military campaign, he exiled his son from his dominions.

"If, within thirty days, I find you anywhere within my kingdom, I shall have you executed," he boomed.

The Queen was terribly distressed. Going at once to Birbal she said: "The Prince would improve if only the Emperor would be less demanding. But to exile his own son on pain of death—it is impossible!"

Birbal thought for a moment. Then he said:

"Send the Prince to me."

When Salim had made his way to Birbal's house, Birbal ordered his servants to make the Prince as comfortable as possible.

"Your Highness can stay here for a few months in secret. Give the King's anger some time to cool. Then let us see."

After a while, Birbal perceived that Akbar regretted banishing his son, although he never spoke of it directly. So he told the Prince:

"Tomorrow morning climb a tree in the Palace garden, and wait until your father and I walk by."

Salim did as he was told. When, in the cool fragrance of morning, Birbal casually directed the King along the garden path which passed that very tree, Akbar chanced to glance up and was at first delighted to lay eyes upon his son—but then he was furious that Salim had dared flaunt his orders.

"What do you think you are doing up there?" shouted Akbar. "Is this foolishness how you hope to redeem my favor?"

"Father," said the Prince, carefully recalling Birbal's instructions, "all these months I have wandered and wandered, trying to reach the frontier and go into exile as you commanded. But however far I went, people always said: 'We too are Akbar's subjects—you must travel far beyond here to reach the limit of his rule.' Finally I despaired of *ever* finding a place where Your Majesty's writ does not run, so I crawled up this tree, thinking that perhaps the only way to leave your vast kingdom is by climbing to Heaven."

Akbar laughed at this witty and flattering apology, and called his son down, receiving him in an embrace of true affection. And, the Queen, in her gratitude, sent Birbal a chest of incomparable pearls.

THE BLIND AND THOSE WHO CANNOT SEE

"The world is full of blind people," said Birbal to the King, "but there are even more who have eyes but cannot understand what they see."

"Birbal himself seems blind," remarked a courtier. "The world is full of people who know perfectly well what they see."

"Can you prove your point?" asked the Emperor.

"Of course," answered Birbal, taking a strip of cloth from his pocket. Winding it around his head, he asked one courtier: "What would you call this?"

"A turban."

Wrapping it around his neck, he turned to a second courtier and asked: "What would you call it now?"

"A scarf."

And wrapping it next around his waist, he turned to a third courtier and inquired:

"Now what is it?"

"A sash," came the reply.

"There you have it," said Birbal to the King. "None of these apparently sighted people can tell the difference between what is essential and what is merely a function of the moment. None of them identified this commonplace object as a piece of cloth."

"A conjurer's trick!" snapped one of the courtiers. "Anybody could have done the same thing for a cheap laugh. But it hardly proves that the world is full of people who are blind."

"Then I will demonstrate it in another way," said Birbal. "if His Majesty will come with me to the main bazaar."

Birbal took the bare frame of a string bed and set it in the middle of the busy market. Then he handed Akbar a ball of string and said: "Do not speak to anyone, but weave the netting across this frame."

Birbal stood by with paper and pen.

The King set to work in the hot sun, and it was not long before astonished passersby began to gather around. At length one of them made bold to ask:

"Sire, what are you doing?"

But the King did not reply. Birbal merely took down the bemused man's name as he went on his way.

Soon another person passed and asked the same question:

"Sire, what are you doing?"

Then another wandered up and enquired:

"Sire, what are you doing?"

And so it went, as word spread through the bazaar of the King's peculiar actions. Generals and noblemen, merchants and paupers, all hurried to put the same question to the Emperor:

"Sire, what are you doing?"

At length, Birbal ran out of paper, but he said:

"That should be enough."

Handing the list to Akbar he said:

"Here are the names of all your subjects who walked up to you while you were weaving the net of a string cot in broad daylight, but still had to *ask* you what you were doing. These are the blind."

Akbar smiled.

"Very well—but what about those who are *not* blind but cannot understand what they see?"

"Sire," grinned Birbal, "it is the same list."

ENDING EVIL

Once, late at night in his elegant House of Worship, the Emperor Akbar mused, "Why doesn't God end poverty and suffering? In my Kingdom, when I want a result, I give an order and I get the result. God is infinitely more powerful than I am. And He is infinitely more good and just. Why doesn't he simply take evil out of the world?"

Birbal smiled, "Because God chooses to work through people, Sire. And we *all* have some evil in us. If He removed evil from the world, *Jahanpanah*, He also would immediately have to take out you and me."

THE MOTHER TONGUE

A stranger applied to the Mughal court for the position of official translator.

"What languages can you speak?" asked the Emperor.

"Persian, Arabic, Sanskrit, Turki, Hebrew, Malay, Chinese, Greek, Portuguese, Dutch, French and English," said the man smugly.

"By Allah!" exclaimed Akbar. "Where is your native place?"

But the man smiled cryptically. "Surely the famous wise men of the Mughal Court can tell you that. A man's speech always reveals his origin."

So Akbar had the court scholars test the stranger in every tongue.

"Your Majesty, he is a master of every language," said one.

"He speaks each language like he was born to it," said another.

"He could come from a dozen countries-his pronunciation is perfect."

"Marvelous," said Akbar. "You will serve me as an ambassador. We can always use able men like you."

"I will not serve Your Majesty unless you can discover my secret. Tell me where I am from, and I will give you a lifetime of loyal service. Otherwise, I will journey to another Court, more deserving of my talents."

Akbar frowned. He disliked not getting something he desired. He turned to Birbal.

"I will need a little time," mused the Wazir. "Please give me until tomorrow."

The interpreter left the palace wreathed in a satisfied smile.

But Birbal took a servant and followed the interpreter to the house where he was lodging. He waited until the dead of night.

When all was still as death, Birbal filtered into the stranger's bed chamber and abruptly threw ice water over his head. The stranger cried out in alarm, but saw only a shadowy figure glide out the door.

The next day at court, the interpreter bowed low before the King, and Birbal calmly announced:

"The stranger is from Gujarat, O Full Moon."

"How did you guess?" cried the stranger.

"I did not guess," smiled Birbal. "It was I who threw water on you in the dead of night. In moments of surprise, or anger, or pain, a man reverts to his mother tongue. I disrupted your slumber, and you cursed me in Gujarati."

The interpreter grinned and bowed to Akbar.

"I hope to live long, O Refuge of the World, and translate the wisdom of Wazir Birbal into many tongues."

THE PHILOSOPHICAL SERVANT

Once Akbar and Birbal were roaming about the city in disguise, when they stayed out too late and the gate of the palace was locked against them. They found a caravanserai, where they decided to spend the night.

Falling asleep in the loft, they were wakened when a trader from Cambay[43] and his servant came in and settled down for the night.

"You sit near the door," said the merchant to his servant, "and keep an eye on my horse tethered outside. Wake me if you see anyone come near him."

"Yes, Master," replied the servant.

Sleep had just begun to weigh upon the eyelids of the merchant, Birbal, and the King, when the servant roused all three, shouting:

"Master! Master!"

"Ho!" shouted the trader, pulling out a dagger. "Get away from my horse—don't touch him!"

"No," said the servant, laying a hand upon the merchant's arm. "No one has come. It is only—I had a thought."

"Well, what is it?" growled the Master, sheathing his knife.

"Well, I have been watching the sky for some time, and I was wondering why, after all these years, it has not fallen down."

"And to tell me *this* you have disturbed my sleep?" exclaimed the trader.

"Well, it did occur to me that there might be pillars somewhere—but then why haven't *they* fallen down?"

"The sky is hung by ropes, so pillars are not needed," snapped the merchant. "Now *you* better go to sleep, and *I* will watch the horse."

"No, no, Master. I could not allow that. You should get your rest."

"Very well." And so he settled down once more upon the straw.

But hardly were the minds of the trader, Birbal, and the King bathed in the sweet fantasies of slumber, when a piercing cry jolted them awake.

"Master! Master!"

"I'll run you through!" howled the trader, bolting out the window in pursuit of imaginary horse thieves . . .

"No, sir—in *here*," called the servant through the open window after him. "I was just thinking . . ."

"*What* were you thinking?" muttered the trader through his teeth as he painfully crawled back over the sill.

"Well, I was just wondering what would happen to the fish if the sea were to catch fire . . ."

"The fish would climb a tree, you idiot! Now, I will never get back to sleep, so we may as well trade shifts."

"I won't hear of it," said the servant. "You are busy man and need your rest."

"Well, try thinking about *that* for a while," said the merchant, falling back into the hay. And though Birbal and Akbar struggled hard to suppress their giggles, at long last sleep spread its velvet wings over all three.

But when the servant pierced the silence of the night again, they sprung like startled pheasants from a field.

"Master! Master!"

"Oh, you are a *terrible* man!" shrieked the shattered merchant. "You have killed my peace, once and for all. Now, quick, quick! No more questions! *You* lay down, while *I* guard the—!" But freezing in his tracks, the trader suddenly wailed at the top of his lungs: "Where is my horse?"

"But *that* is what I wanted to ask *you*, Master," the servant explained. "Is there really any point in *either* of us staying awake, now that the horse is gone?"

Akbar and Birbal could hold their sides no longer. They burst into gales of laughter.

"Thieves! Hooligans! Devils! Fools!" screamed the merchant, deliriously drawing his sword.

But Akbar leapt from the loft and said:

"Peace upon you, man. I am Akbar, and I hereby pledge you a *dozen* horses in compensation—for my friend and I have seldom passed a merrier night!"

A FAIR-WEATHER FRIEND

Akbar was worried, as usual, about his son, Prince Salim. He told a group of friends:

"Salim spends all his time flirting and getting drunk on wine. It is disgraceful. And he has no respect for me. If I am not careful, one day he will try to take the Crown from my own head."

"Not possible," cried some of the nobles.

"He's a fine boy," said others.

"He has the best father in the world," said the rest.

"His father has nothing to do with it," snapped Akbar. "The problem is that worthless young noble he runs with."

"Ah," said Birbal, "you mean that young ruffian, Nasib."

"Exactly," frowned the Emperor. "If only I could separate Salim from such bad influences as Nasib. But how?"

"Nothing could be simpler," smiled one of the courtiers. "Exile Nasib and his whole family."

"What if Salim followed?" said Akbar. "You know how stubborn a fifteen-year old can be."

"Forbid him to see Nasib again," said another courtier.

"That would only turn Salim against me," said the King.

"If you really want to separate them, Sire" said Birbal, "call both boys into the Hall of Public Audience tomorrow and do exactly as I say."

Akbar smiled. The next day, he sent for the two young men, who felt terribly important coming before the King.

After handling some weighty affairs of state, Akbar turned to Nasib and said:

"Young man, approach me."

Nasib glanced at Prince Salim. Both of them started toward the throne, but Akbar held up a hand.

"Not Prince Salim," he said. "Only Nasib."

The prince turned red, but stopped in his tracks. Nasib approached the Great Mughal, trembling. Akbar put his lips close to Nasib's ear and whispered:

"A mango has a single seed."

Nasib stood up, clearly puzzled. But the Emperor nodded, and the young man backed away from the throne.

When *durbar* was over, Prince Salim rushed to Nasib and gripped his arm.

"What did the Emperor say to you?"

"Nothing," said Nasib.

"Nothing?" cried Prince Salim. "That is not possible. He whispered something to you in front of the whole court. It had to be important. What did he say?"

"He really said nothing that made sense," said Nasib.

"You are lying!" shouted Prince Salim. "The Emperor is my father, and if you are my friend, you will not keep his secret from me!"

"How dare you call me a liar?" yelled Nasib. "If you must know, the King told me that there is only one seed in a mango."

"Do you take me for a fool?" hissed Prince Salim. "Tell me the truth, or I'll punch you in the nose."

"That is the truth," cried Nasib.

"All right, you asked for it." And Prince Salim struck Nasib in the face.

Nasib was about to hit the prince back, when he noticed Birbal standing nearby. Rubbing his nose, he said, "You're crazy, Salim. I never want to see your face again."

"If you do, it will be too soon for me," shouted Prince Salim. And he stormed over to Birbal.

"How could my father trust an idiot like Nasib?" he fumed.

"I suppose your father trusted him," said Birbal, "because he is your friend."

"Well, you can tell my father that Nasib is my worst enemy now," said Prince Salim.

But Birbal put a fatherly arm around the prince's shoulders and said,

"My son, your worst enemy is the man who chooses your fair-weather friends."

"But *I* choose my friends . . ." said Salim.

"I *mean* you," smiled Birbal.

"In other words," smiled Salim, "geese fly in flocks; eagles soar alone."

"Well said," replied the Wazir.

And when Akbar heard the result, he gave Birbal a purse of gold and Salim the command of one thousand knights.

THE TIBETAN MONKS

Two Tibetan monks arrived in Fatehpur Sikri, bald as marble and wearing saffron cloaks. They threaded the lively streets of the bazaar until they found the open stall of a little old jeweler, known throughout the city for his fair-dealing. Bowing low, the Tibetans said:

"Respected sir, we have made the long journey from the Roof of the World, bringing rare ornaments of turquoise and virgin silver. Would you like to buy them?"

"After so long a trek," smiled the old man, "you must be footsore. Please be seated in my shop and let my assistant bring you spiced milk, while I examine this elegant jewelry."

Sitting on the goldsmith's crisp linen cushions, the monks peered with beady eyes at the old man's expressions as he turned the ornaments over and over in his hands.

"Beautiful, indeed," he smiled at last. "But their style is strange to me, and I cannot say at once what they may be worth. Will you leave them with me overnight? I will speak to my brothers in the jewelry guild and give you a fair estimate of what they will fetch anywhere in Sikri."

The monks nodded, and the old man told his attendant to make them a receipt, but they interrupted him at once.

"We do not require a receipt. We trust you. But you must promise one thing—do not return the jewels to either one of us alone—only give them back if we both come together."

The old man raised his eyebrows. "Strange," he thought, "that two monks who have journeyed so far together should mistrust each other." But aloud he said:

"As you wish."

The next morning one of the monk's came early to the jeweler's shop.

"Ah, good news, friend," smiled the old man. "Your jewelry was very well received. I think you will be happy with the high price people here will pay. In fact, I am prepared to buy them from you myself."

"You have been most kind," said the monk. "But we have decided not to sell the ornaments. Please return them to me now."

Now the jeweler narrowed his eyes.

"Didn't you tell me not to give them back unless both of you were present? Where is the monk who owns the other half of these?"

"There, sir," said the first monk, pointing at a bald and saffron-clad figure at a baker's shop down the road. "We must leave the city today, and he is getting provisions. But surely you can see we are both here."

"Fair enough," chuckled the old man, "but if you ever do want to sell these, please remember me."

"We will," said the monk, taking the ornaments and tucking them into his cloak. But the jeweler did not notice that he then wandered off in the direction opposite to his companion.

Scarcely a quarter of an hour had passed when the second monk presented himself at the goldsmith's shop and said:

"Good morning, sir. Have you seen my friend?"

"Seen him?" said the old man. "Why you saw him yourself when he was right here a few minutes ago and I gave him the jewelry."

"What!" shouted the second monk, dropping his parcel of fresh, hot bread. "But I have just spoken with him and he is waiting for me at the city gates. He told *me* to get the jewelry back. You are holding out on us! Fraud! Thief!"

The jeweler could do nothing to calm the hysterical monk, and to his great humiliation a crowd quickly gathered. In all his years the little old jeweler had never been called dishonest.

But as luck would have it, that very morning Birbal was headed for the jeweler's shop to have a golden necklace mended for his daughter. Seeing the commotion, he asked the people for enough silence to hear the monk and the goldsmith out.

Noting the respect with which the merchants treated Birbal, the monk guessed he was an officer of the King and watched him narrowly from the corner of his eye. But he kept a bold face. "This man is a liar," he hissed. "He has cheated us shrewdly. If he will not return our jewelry, he should be made to pay."

"Pay!" cried the jeweler. "So that's your trick! You lend your jewelry, get it back, and then extort payment for it! Who knows how many times it has been sold!"

Now Birbal accepted a hot tumbler of spiced milk from someone and sipped it, rubbing his chin. At last he said:

"Your friend cannot have gone far. And it should not be difficult for the Imperial guards to pick up a bald Tibetan monk in the streets of Fatehpur Sikri. However, if you will catch up to your friend and bring him to this shop, the jeweler shall be made to return your ornaments, as he promised. But he cannot, of course, do this until both of you are present, as agreed."

"But, sir," protested the jeweler.

"On pain of death!" said Birbal sternly.

With his eyes flicking nervously from side to side, the monk stood for a moment, deep in thought:

"This Birbal holds me in his custody now but hopes to trick me into also letting him trap my friend."

Aloud he muttered:

"We shall both be back within the hour."

And he wended his way through the crowd, disappearing round the corner. Although the people and the goldsmith passed an anxious hour, neither monk was ever heard from again.

"Now," smiled Birbal calmly, "about this necklace I need repaired . . ."

LOYALTY

Akbar loved philosophical questions. One evening, in the Hall of Worship, he posed Birbal a challenge:

"What is loyalty but gratitude for service? How can we define it? I would like to meet the most loyal and the least grateful creatures in my kingdom, Birbal. Bring them to *durbar* tomorrow."

"Your wish is my command, Brightest Eminence," said Birbal.

At home Birbal sat upon his terrace and looked out over the garden, rubbing his temples. His daughter came to bring him a glass of rosewater.

"Are you troubled, father?" she asked.

"A little," answered Birbal. And he explained the Emperor's challenge.

"Father," smiled the girl. "That is no problem at all. Go to sleep. I will give you the answer in the morning."

Birbal smiled. His daughter was so like him.

When Birbal arose the next morning and got ready for court, he asked his daughter:

"What is the answer to my problem, child?"

"All you have to do is take my husband and our dog Lal to court with you. They are the answer to the riddle."

"But of course!" laughed Birbal. "I should have thought of that before!"

When Birbal entered the *durbar* with a dog, the Emperor was shocked.

"Birbal," he said, "where is your respect?"

"I am only following your orders, Your Majesty. This dog is a mongrel, but no one is more loyal."

"You are right," laughed Akbar. "A dog is more loyal than a man's shadow. But what about the most ungrateful creature?"

"Here," said Birbal, pointing to his daughter's husband.

"But that is your son-in-law," said the Emperor.

"Yes, Your Majesty. However much you give a son-in-law, he still resents it."

"You are right," laughed the King. "So we must reward the dog and punish the son-in-law. What do you suggest?"

"We should give the dog a sumptuous feast," said Birbal.

"And the son-in-law?" asked Akbar.

"We should forgive him, *Jahanpanah*. Unless you or I can honestly say we are more grateful to our fathers-in-law than this wretch is to his."

"I could not honestly say it," laughed the Emperor. And he sent Birbal and his two companions home with lavish rewards.

THE PRACTICAL BEGGAR

One day, as the Emperor and Birbal wandered through Fatehpur Sikri in disguise, the King noticed two beggars.

One beggar cried out, "O God, send me money!"

Another beggar cried out, "O King, send me food!"

Akbar said to Birbal: "The second beggar makes sense. At least he calls to *me*, and I can answer his prayer. But whoever saw God sending money to a beggar?"

"God works through people, *Huzur*. And no person can fathom the ways of God."

"Maybe," said Akbar. "But I will reward the *sensible* beggar."

He told Birbal to prepare a heaping platter of lamb pilaf. At the very bottom of the mountain of rice, Akbar concealed twelve gold *mohurs*. Then he had the platter delivered to the practical beggar.

The next day he went to see what effect his lesson had produced.

The beggar who had been appealing to God was gone. The practical beggar was in his usual spot, but now he too was praying, "O God, send me money!"

Irritated, Akbar asked, "Where is your friend?"

The beggar replied, "A miracle happened, sir. Somehow God answered his prayers and sent my friend a fortune. Now he lives in magnificent style and has left his begging spot to me."

Birbal asked, "But why have *you* stopped praying to the King? Didn't *he* answer your prayer?"

"Oh, yes," said the beggar. "The King sent me a great platter of food."

"What was in it?" asked Akbar.

"A wonderful feast," said the beggar. "Lamb, rice, raisins, spices . . ."

"Anything else?" asked Birbal.

"Oh, I don't know," shrugged the beggar. "It was far too much. Once I had eaten half, I gave the rest to my neighbor, the other beggar."

Akbar's jaw dropped. Birbal smiled and pointed respectfully heavenward.

"God knows the end, Sire, from the beginning."[44]

THE GOLDEN TOUCH

An old widow and her daughter-in-law came to see Birbal at his house.

"Birbal *Sahib*, you are kind and just. Please have pity on two poor women."

"Sit down," said Birbal gently. And he gestured to some servants, who brought the ladies spiced milk. After he had waited a polite while, Birbal said:

"Tell me how I may help."

"My son," said the old woman, "was a soldier in the Imperial army. He served the Emperor for years. He fought from the glaciers of the Hindu Kush to the steaming marshes of Bengal. He often did not see his wife, my daughter-in-law here, for many months. His child was born while he was away, and then he made the supreme sacrifice for the Emperor. My son lost his life in the great battle of Haldighati[45]."

"Your grandchild will be proud of his father's glory," said Birbal softly. "But why have you come to me?"

"*Huzur*, we have no money. All that my son left to his wife and child is this sword, scarred in battle."

Birbal took the sword and looked that the many traces of hard fighting etched upon it. This man *had* been a brave soldier. He said:

"Our Emperor is as generous as he is kind. Come to *durbar* tomorrow. Then do as I say." And Birbal gave the old woman instructions.

The next day in the Hall of Public Audience, the old lady petitioned for a word with the King. Akbar said:

"Come forward. We will hear her request."

"*Jahanpanah*," she said, "my son wielded this weapon many times in battles to bring glory to your name. But at Haldighati he gave his life for his country. Please, Sire, give my son's sword an honored place in the royal armory."

The King accepted the sword and examined it. To one of the courtiers standing nearby, he said, "It is old and badly beaten up. What use would it be in the royal armory? Give the old lady five golden coins."

Birbal overheard the order. "Only five?" he said.

The King frowned. "Do you question its worth?"

"May I see the sword, Your Majesty?"

"Certainly," said the King, handing it carelessly to Birbal.

"Ah," said Birbal, holding the blade up to the light. "Hmm," he murmured, turning it around. "Oh," he muttered, squinting one eye and examining it like a jeweler.

The Emperor asked:

"What can you possibly find so fascinating about that worthless old sword?"

"Ah," smiled Birbal. "I am waiting to see it turn to gold."

"What!" blurted Akbar. "Why on earth should it turn to gold?"

"Well, of course it will," said Birbal impatiently. "The Greeks had an ancient king, Midas, and everything *he* touched turned to gold. But Midas was nothing compared to you, O Shadow of God Upon the Earth. The touch of so generous a king as yourself will, surely, turn this sword of a soldier's honor into gold that shines forever in the memories of men."

"Ah," said the King and thought a moment. Then he said, "You remind me, Birbal, that a reputation for generosity is worth more than gold."

Turning to his Treasurer, the Emperor said, "Give the old woman a thousand gold *mohurs* with royal thanks for the noble son she has given to our country."

THE PILFERING TAILOR

"**Y**ou cannot generalize about people," said Akbar during a certain discussion with Birbal. "Every individual is unique."

Birbal disagreed.

"People can be surprisingly easy to predict," he said.

"Give me an example," said the King.

"Very well: take the question of honesty. A trader, a goldsmith, and a tailor never should be trusted."

"How so?" asked Akbar.

Birbal smiled. "Because a merchant will always overcharge for the goods he sells, a goldsmith will always pretend that the gold he is filching from a client has been lost in fashioning jewelry, and a tailor will always help himself to a piece of his customer's cloth."

"But I feel," objected the Emperor, "that honesty can be *created*. A person who is aware of these things can be alert enough to prevent them. Take the example of the tailor. Instead of leaving the cloth *with* him, suppose you had him stitch the garment under your very nose?"

"It is an age-old profession," grinned Birbal. "Every tailor will find a way."

"Let us try," said the King. And he called for a length of precious silk which had been sent to him by the King of Burma. It was so rare and fine that the entire bolt could be drawn through the eye of a ring.

"There is no match for this in your Kingdom," said Birbal, admiring the silk. "At least we can be sure the tailor will be tempted."

So they called the Queen's favorite tailor and commissioned him to make a blouse for Her Majesty.

"But there is one condition," added Birbal. "You must do your work here behind a guarded door. This is to prevent your stealing any of this rare cloth."

"Sir!" cried the tailor, scandalized. "I come from a long line of tailors who have served the royal family. It would be unthinkable of me to stoop so low."

"Nevertheless," said Birbal. "That is the condition."

"Just give me time to go home and fetch my tools," said the tailor and left the Palace.

When he returned he was shown to a private chamber flanked by two fierce-looking guards. Handling the fabulous cloth with delight, he set about his task.

Evening had come, and the tailor still was hard at work, when his little boy came to see him. The guards let the lad pass without question.

"Father," said the child. "When are you coming home?"

"I cannot leave until I finish," said the tailor, "and I think this will take me at least until tomorrow."

"Ha!" shouted the boy. "Mother says this is why we are so poor—because you take such a long time to sew a single blouse."

The tailor's face went purple with rage.

"You impudent waif!" he shouted. He took off his shoe and hurled it after the boy. "Remember who you are talking to!"

The boy dodged the slipper gaily and picked it up.

"Now I will take this to Mother," he taunted, "and *you* will have to walk home with one foot bare!"

With his father muttering curses, the boy ran off in peals of laughter—leaving even the guards to chuckle into their whiskers.

When the tailor presented the blouse the following day, the Queen was charmed.

"Is any of the Burmese silk left over?" asked the King before handing the tailor his pay.

"If it were, Sire, I would surely have returned it. We tailors are all honest, although the tongues of rumor-mongers paint our reputations black."

Akbar laughed and sent the tailor on his way.

"You see, Birbal?" said the King. "Whatever might have been in his heart, we *made* him into an honest man."

"Let us wait to pass judgment," said Birbal.

"You are a poor loser—or suspicious by nature," replied Akbar. "But let it be."

After a few days, however, one of the Queen's maids reported that she had seen a woman in the bazaar wearing a blouse exactly like Her Majesty's. The *Begum* complained to the King.

"I thought that cloth was a gift from Burma, woven especially for me."

When Akbar told Birbal of this, he had the tailor summoned.

"On pain of death," thundered the Wazir, "confess you are a thief!"

Knowing Birbal's reputation, the tailor sunk to his knees:

"Oh, sir, pardon this erring soul!"

"I may deal leniently with you, if you explain to the Emperor how you pilfered that cloth."

The tailor gulped and could not raise his eyes from terror.

"I gave my son instructions to come and told him what to say, my lord—and then hid the material in my shoe. I threw it after the lad, and he smuggled it home."

"You will have to be punished for your dishonesty," said the Emperor, shaking his head. "But I am inclined to make the sentence light; for Birbal has amply shown me—some things are in the nature of man."

AKBAR PROVES A POINT

Akbar recognized that Birbal had made many enemies among the jealous flatterers at Court. Usually, he simply ignored this, enjoying his favorite companion's merry fellowship unhindered. But sometimes the whispering and back-biting annoyed him to the point where he could stand it no longer.

One day, when yet another rumor-mongering courtier was asking the King how he could depend so much on the advice of a country fellow who was, after all, no more than a clever jester, Akbar decided to make a demonstration.

Calling Birbal and all his worst enemies together, he informed them that a caravan of merchants had just camped outside the city walls. He told them to go out and bring him news about the strangers.

Puzzled, the courtiers cantered out in great haughtiness and style. They surveyed the encampment of travelers, and, observing nothing unusual, returned to the Palace.

"Well?" asked Akbar. "What have you discovered?"

The scheming courtiers hardly knew what to say.

"It was just a normal caravan, Sire . . . nothing special at all."

"Well, how many were in it, for example?"

The courtiers glanced at each other blankly.

"Twenty or so, somewhere about there," murmured one.

"Ah. And what were they trading?"

"Trading, Sire?" gulped another courtier.

"Yes!" snapped the Emperor. "Did I not send you for information?"

"Cloth!" yelped one of the noblemen helplessly.

"And spices and oil," chimed in a second.

"And grain," mumbled a third.

"What were they riding?"

"Ah! Horses!" said someone, proudly.

"No camels?" asked Akbar.

"Oh, yes, some camels. Of course, there *would* be camels."

"How many?" demanded the King.

The courtiers felt their throats going dry. How on earth could they have thought to count the camels?

"Round about dozen, Sire," guessed one.

"Do you have anything else to offer from this wealth of information?" sneered the King.

Wretchedly, they shook their heads.

"Birbal!" thundered the Great Mughal.

"Command, O Celestial Highness."

"Tell me what *you* observed."

"I noticed a caravan of twenty-seven merchants, Sire. All but four were mounted on mares. Of these twelve were brown, three were black, six were brown and white, and two were white. The remaining four men were riding mules. They had thirteen camels, and one was lame in the left foreleg. Their wares consisted of silks from China, mustard oil and saffron from Kashmir, European muskets from the Portuguese trading post in Gujarat, pearls from Dubai, and aromatic woods from Yemen."

"Anything else?"

"They are headed for Bengal, and wish Your Majesty long life."

Akbar turned to the assembled Court.

"I show favoritism to no man," he told them. "But any adviser with so keen an eye, you must agree, has, to a King, a price above rubies."

The Loveliest Child

When Akbar's grandchild, Prince Khurram, was born, the Emperor could think of nothing else.

"Is he not the loveliest child you have ever seen?" Akbar asked a group of his closest friends.

"By far," answered some.

"Without a doubt," said the others.

But Birbal did not utter a word.

"Birbal," frowned the King. "Don't you agree?"

"It is a difficult question, O Light of the World. What test is there for real beauty?"

"Well," said Akbar, exasperated. "You would not call a rose ugly, would you? Or a crow beautiful?"

Birbal smiled.

"You have a point."

But the Emperor was not satisfied.

"You seem unconvinced," he said to Birbal. "Very well, we shall have a test. Tomorrow each of you shall bring a beautiful child to dinner. We shall see how they compare to Prince Khurram."

The next evening, the King's friends all complied with his instructions. But as Akbar looked the little ones over, he remarked:

"This one's eyes seem a bit close together. And *that* one there is a little too fat. I still think Khurram outshines them all."

Then he noticed Birbal had not brought a child, and he demanded to know why.

"*Maharaj*, the child *I* found is truly the most beautiful in all of Fatehpur Sikri, but his mother will not let him leave her sight, for fear of the evil eye. If you want to see the boy, we shall have to visit him—in disguise."

"All right," said Akbar dryly. "I am curious to see this precious star of infant beauty."

The next morning, dressed as ordinary citizens, the Emperor and a small group of friends followed Birbal through the twisting streets of the bazaar. They went a long way, finally passing out through the city gates.

"Where are you taking us?" said Akbar. "To Qandahar?"

"Patience, *Huzur*," smiled Birbal. And they carried on, while the houses grew shabbier and smaller, and the streets narrowed down to filthy camel tracks.

At long last, Birbal halted across from a thatched shack and said:

"That is where the boy lives, my lord. But we must watch him from a distance."

"Truly gems are sometimes found in the mud," muttered Akbar. But even as he spoke, the door of the hut creaked open and a half-naked little urchin toddled out.

"Ah, there," said Birbal with satisfaction, "is the most beautiful child in Sikri!"

All eyes turned in astonishment toward the scrawny mean-looking, cross-eyed waif—who happily sat down in a puddle and began covering himself with mud.

"Is this one of your pranks?" demanded the Emperor. "That is the ugliest child I have ever seen!"

But just then the lad pricked his finger on a potsherd and let out the miserable howl of a wounded hyena. From the wretched shack his mother burst out and scooped the baby up in her arms.

"Sweetheart, my angel," she cooed. "I'll throw that potsherd in the fire for having hurt my darling, my moon."

"How can she love this ugly child?" wondered one of the Emperor's friends aloud. "Imagine calling that little hooligan the Moon!"

Suddenly the woman picked up a clod of mud and flung it at the nobles.

"What did you say?" she shrieked. "I heard that—you, you—peasant! You must be blind or stupid to say such lies! Go and search all of Hindustan—you will never find a lovelier child than my Deshmukh! Now get out of my sight, before I give all of you loafers a proper thrashing!"

Beating a hasty retreat, the Great Mughal dusted off his turban and remarked:

"Birbal, I see your point—in its parents' eyes every child surpasses the beauty of the moon!"

"And even royal grandparents," smiled Birbal, "see things pretty much the same . . ."

WHY THE RIVER JUMNA WEEPS

Akbar used to lie awake at night, hearing the purling of the River Jumna beyond his balcony, far below.

When the rains came and adorned the grateful earth with emeralds, the river swelled and murmured all the more—and the night grew vibrant with the chattering of frog songs and of rain. Then it almost seemed to the thoughtful King that the River Jumna wept.

When he next met his friend Birbal he asked:

"Why should this be so?"

Birbal pondered for a moment and then replied:

"I think, Sire, it is because she leaves the home of her Father Mountain and goes to the abode of Ocean, who claims her as his bride."

And the two stood listening to the drifting veils of rain on the silvery whirlpools, as the river rolled on its way.

THE LEGEND OF
BIRBAL ENDURES

So Birbal served Akbar, and Akbar served the people of India for many years. As the tales of these two clever and compassionate men were told from the frozen Hindu Kush to the palm-lined shores of Bengal while they lived, they continue to be told, as a delight for children and a lesson for adults, down to the present day.

THE END OF BIRBAL

B irbal was killed in battle when he was leading a difficult expedition against the Afghans in 1586. Rumors spread that his fall was due to treachery. Perhaps the jealous courtiers at last had their revenge.

When Akbar learned of Birbal's death, he took no food for two days and two nights. Overwhelmed with grief, the King blurted out this lament:

> *O Birbal,*
> *To the helpless you never brought harm.*
> *You gave them all that you had.*
> *O friend, who now will be my right arm,*
> *Since you leave me so helpless and sad?*

Birbal's beautiful home may still be seen in the abandoned city of Fatehpur Sikri, near Agra. This domed, two-story house is a lovely example of structural and decorative harmony in a residence of Mughal times.

ENDNOTES

1   Great king
2   "Refuge of the world," a favorite title for the Great Mughal.
3   Princess (Turkish)
4   Lord (Arabic)
5   Serene Presence (Turkish), like the title of the near-contemporary French prince de Condé's, "Most Serene Highness"
6   Milady the Queen
7   Court, hall, council chamber (Persian)
8   Court (Persian)
9   Penny (one hundredth of a rupee—Hindi)
10   King of kings
11   A gold coin worth fifteen rupees
12   Mackerel
13   Flat bread
14   The Deccan is a vast plateau, encompassing most of Central and Southern India. Deccan is the Anglicized form of the Prakrit *dakkhin*, derived from the Sanskrit *dakshina*, meaning south.
15   In Islam a mullah is a learned man, a teacher, or a doctor of religious law (*Sharia*); from Arabic *mawla* (master, friend).
16   An ascetic holy man
17   A Hindu religious mendicant or ascetic
18   Margosa tree, a fast-growing broad-leaved evergreen, native to India and Myanmar (Burma)
19   A mendicant ascetic (Persian), or Muslim monk, often a source of wisdom, medicine, poetry, enlightenment, and wit
20   Father (Hindi), often a title for Indian feudal lords
21   From *mausem* (Arabic), meaning season; monsoons are the Indian Ocean trade winds, which blow from the southwest in summer and from the northeast in winter.

The winter monsoons, coming from the plains, keep the sky a cloudless blue and the land dry for months on end. The summer sea breezes bring months of heavy, tropical rainfall.

22   Homemade cheese

23   One of the two great Sanskrit epics of ancient India (the other is the *Ramayana*); the title means "Great India," or "Epic of the Bharata Dynasty," Bharata being the legendary king who founded the realm of Bharat (India). Indian governments today still use Bharat as an official synonym for "India."

24   Memoirs of Akbar

25   Contributed by James A. Moseley, MD

26   A region in northwest Arabia, home of the holy city of Mecca

27   The Ka'aba is a large building shaped like a cube. (The name Ka'aba, and the English word *cube*, both come from the Arabic word meaning cube.) One of the Ka'aba's cornerstones, "the Black Stone," is allegedly a meteor. The Ka'aba was once a temple for idols and pre-dates Muhammad, but it is now the holiest place in Islam.

28   A spring near the Ka'aba, said to be the source of life-giving water that can satisfy hunger and thirst and cure illness.

29   Rose water (Persian)

30   A common greeting, meaning "I humbly bow to you" (Sanskrit), usually said with the palms pressed together and held under the chin, as if in prayer.

31   Strong spirits distilled from fermented fruits, grains, sugarcane, palm sap or coconuts

32   A region comprising parts of northeastern Afghanistan and Tajikistan, famous for its rubies

33   A city founded in 1488 in northwestern Rajasthan in western India, along the ancient Silk Road

34   The beautiful capital of Kashmir, founded by King Pravarasena over 2,000 years ago, on the banks of the Jhelum and Lake Dal

35   A person blessed with knowledge, talent, ability or fortune

36   One of Pakistan's four provinces today, the cradle of ancient civilizations on the subcontinent; when British General Charles Napier conquered Sind in 1843, *Punch* magazine reported that he sent a single-word telegram to London, announcing his victory with the pun: "*Peccavi*," Latin for "I have sinned."

37   The sacred fig or bo tree, considered holy by Hindus, Buddhists, and Jains; Prince Siddhartha was sitting under a bo tree when he found enlightenment (*bodhi*) and became the Buddha ("the enlightened one"). This same bo tree, adorned with prayer flags chattering in the humid breeze, still stands today.

38   Chess is an Anglicization of the Persian word *shah* (king), although the name of the game in Persian is *shatranj*. The term checkmate comes from *shah mat*, meaning "The King is ambushed (Persian)," not "The King is dead (Arabic)".

[39] Tribes of Iranian origin who live in the arid Baluchistan plateau of southeast Iran, southern Afghanistan, and southwest Pakistan

[40] Pundit means a learned man, schooled in the spiritual scriptures of India. The suffix -ji is an additional term of respect.

[41] A dish of mixed lentils, potatoes, onions, coconut, spices and rice

[42] Fakir (Arabic) means a spiritual miracle-maker or a common street beggar who chants holy names, scriptures or verses. Stereotypes include near-naked mystics who walk barefoot on burning coals, levitate during meditation, or "live on air" (fast).

[43] Cambay, also known as Khambhat, is a town in Gujarat State, India. Marco Polo mentioned it in 1293. It was an important trading center, until its harbor gradually silted up.

[44] This story contributed by Balik Hadadian.

[45] Haldighati is a pass in the Aravalli Mountains of Rajasthan in western India. Its name comes from the region's turmeric-colored soil. (Turmeric is *haldi* in Hindi.) In 1576 at Haldighati Akbar defeated the Rana Pratap Singh of Mewar.

Made in the USA
Monee, IL
01 June 2020